Rico Stays

Rico Stays

Pigeon-Blood Red Book 3

Ed Duncan

For my siblings, Minnie (Brady), Attwood, Jr., Bobbie, David, and Christopher

Chapter One

It was a nice day for a ballgame: sunny and mild in the mid-seventies with a slight breeze blowing in from left field. Rico inhaled, appreciating the sweet scent of steaming hot dogs that hung in the air just above the stadium seats.

"Here we go. Into the bottom of the seventh, all tied up one to one. This has turned into a dandy."

Rico opened his eyes. It was a nice day for a ballgame, all right, but he was watching it on TV from his favorite easy chair. There were no hotdogs. He had closed his eyes for a second between innings and had drifted away, only to be ushered back to wakefulness by the practiced cadence of the announcer's voice.

"Oh, well," he said to himself out loud. "Time for a beer." He rose and as he did, his phone rang. It was his land line, a relic he knew, but after so many years, he couldn't bear to part with it. Almost no one called him on it except telemarketers and, of course, his stunningly attractive girlfriend, Jean. Along with the remote, the phone rested on a small side table next to his chair. He glanced at the caller I.D., grabbed the remote, and lowered the volume on the TV. He picked up the phone and eased back down into his chair. "Hit me," he said.

"Still watching the game?" Jean asked, on the other end.

"Yeah."

"Close game?"

"Right again."

"I guess it wouldn't be the best time to ask for a favor then."

"Three out of three," he said.

"What if I asked *real nice*?" she teased.

"That wouldn't help," Rico said.

Jean frowned and rolled her eyes. "Rico –"

"But I'll come and get you anyway."

"Read my mind again," Jean said.

"It doesn't take Sherlock Holmes to figure out you bought more than you and the old guy could carry. Do me a favor. Next time take the car."

"Well, I would have if I'd known. But it's such a beautiful day and –"

"Hold it," Rico interrupted, staring at the TV, and turning the volume up.

In the background the announcer roared, *"A swing and a miss! Struck him out!"*

"Listen," Rico said. "If you're ready now, I'll come and get you, okay?"

"We'll be ready – Sherlock."

He started to tell her gently what she could do with the Sherlock comment, but she had already disconnected. He smiled to himself and shook his head in mock exasperation. He glanced at his watch and calculated how long it would take to drive to the supermarket and back. If he was lucky, he figured he could make it back in time to see the end of the game. In the meantime, he could listen on the car radio.

Rico stood and headed for the door. As he reached it and started to turn the knob, he hesitated. He was missing something he almost always carried with him. He turned around and his eyes focused on a straight back chair, an arm's length away from his easy chair. On it hung a powder-blue shoulder holster, inside of which rested a .45 Sig Sauer P226 automatic. He had thought about replacing it with the newer 320, but there was nothing wrong with his trusty 226. When he got rid of his land line, maybe he would think about trading up to the 320. He had heard that the Navy Seals were finally switching from Sig Sauers to Glocks, to bring them in line with the rest of the Navy and the other branches of the Armed Services. He thought that was a mistake. The Glock and the Sig are both fine, reliable pistols and most shooters would be hard pressed to distinguish between the two where accuracy is concerned. But Rico wasn't most shooters and he could tell the difference.

He lingered another moment, then checked his watch again. It was too nice a day to wear a jacket. Besides, he was just going a few blocks and would only have to get out of the car for a minute or two to help Jean with the groceries. "What the hell," he said out loud. He turned the door knob the rest of the way and walked out.

Minutes later he exited his apartment building, donning his ever-present aviator sunglasses as he walked out into the bright sunlight. He was a big man, athletic and tall, with a long, confident stride. His car was parked on the street about a three-minute walk away. Once inside, he started the car and turned the radio on to the station broad-casting the game.

"...*Bottom of the eighth... Still tied one to one...*"

As Rico neared the supermarket a few minutes later, he noticed a group of pre-teens playing baseball in a field across the street from the supermarket. They reminded him of the days he used to play the game with a motley crew of kids in his old neighborhood. Even at twelve or thirteen, he was a crack outfielder and could hit the ball a mile. The kid at the plate today looked like a pretty good hitter, too. Rico could tell by his fluid practice swings and the way, holding the bat, he cocked his wrists at his waist and planted his feet deep in the imaginary batter's box.

Still admiring the boy's batting stance, Rico pulled into the super-market parking lot and slowed his car to a crawl so he could watch the first pitch. The boy took a vicious cut and whiffed.

Meanwhile, the game continued on the radio. "*... Bases loaded... And the pitch...*" But by now the announcer's voice was only back-ground noise for the game across the street, as Rico stopped the car and watched. The batter swung hard at the next pitch and missed badly again. '*Take your time, kid,*' he thought.

Exiting the store, Jean spied Rico's car stopped just inside the parking lot. Pushing a shopping cart loaded with groceries, she waved and headed in his direction. Rico saw her and nodded. Then he nosed his car into a nearby parking space facing the game across the street.

The announcer on the radio droned on. *"... Top of the ninth ... All knotted up at one to one ..."*

Leaving the radio on, Rico turned the ignition off and peered across the street. The same batter was at the plate. He didn't swing at the next pitch. *'Good eye,'* Rico said to himself. The boy swung hard at the next one and connected this time, lifting a towering fly ball high over the left fielder's head toward the street in front of the supermarket. Shorter and thinner than the muscular batter, the left fielder was fast on his feet. He gave chase as the ball drifted beyond the field and over the street toward the supermarket. Keeping one eye on the ball and the other on traffic (which was mercifully light), the outfielder continued his pursuit to the edge of the field and then across the street.

Arriving at the parking lot about midway between Rico's car and where Jean was standing twenty yards away, the boy timed his leap perfectly, reached up and speared the ball, which lodged precariously in the top of the webbing of his glove, half in and half out.

And then there was a sickening thud. His momentum had caused him to collide with a skinny young man with greasy dark hair, who was carrying a brown paper grocery bag filled with bottles of liquor of almost every variety – gin, bourbon, Scotch, rye, and rum – purchased for a party that night. The man, Larry Cosgrove, had seen the boy an instant before the collision, too late to avoid it but soon enough to brace himself against it. The boy bounced off Cosgrove's hip and tumbled to the ground, but with the resilience of youth, he rolled over once and instantly sprang to his feet, still holding the ball in his glove. Grinning, he thrust the glove high above his head in triumph.

Cosgrove managed to absorb the blow and maintain his balance, but he couldn't save his precious cargo. The bag flew out of his arms and on to the asphalt pavement, smashing all the bottles inside. With his back to the boy, Cosgrove, barely containing his rage, stood staring at the beige rivulets of liquor seeping from the wet paper bag.

The boy had been too preoccupied to notice the bottles crash against the pavement, but when he saw the liquor escaping from what was left of the paper bag, his joy at holding on to the ball rapidly dissipated and turned to dread. His first instinct was to take off back across the street as fast as his legs would carry him. Instead, his home training kicked in and, head down, he slowly approached Cosgrove, stopping a few feet away. "I'm sorry, mister," he said meekly. "I didn't see you."

Cosgrove – who hadn't had any home training – turned to face him. "No shit," he sneered and took one menacing step toward the boy, whose initial urge to run returned, but before he could act on it, Cosgrove reached out and, with both hands against the boy's chest, shoved him violently to the ground. "Did you see that?" he taunted.

The boy landed hard on his rear and slid a foot or so on the asphalt. The pavement stung and he wanted to cry, but he held it in. When he answered, though, his voice was a whimper. "I said I was sorry, mister."

Cosgrove moved toward him and stood straddling him as he lay on his back, propped up on his elbows. "Why the fuck didn't you watch where you were goin'?"

The boy said nothing but this time, despite his best efforts, he couldn't completely hold back his tears, and he raised a hand to his face to hide them. Still brooding, Cosgrove stepped to one side but continued to hover nearby, not sure yet of his next move. The boy was petrified, too intimidated to move.

By now a small knot of onlookers had gathered around, including some of the other baseball players who had made their way across the street. Jean saw the collision but not its aftermath, because the growing crowd blocked her view. But Gabriel Koblentz, Jean's elderly neighbor and shopping companion (whom Rico referred to as "the old guy"), saw the whole thing. He had left the store after she did, but free of the shopping cart, he had walked on a little ahead.

Koblentz didn't know what else, if anything, Cosgrove had in mind, but he felt sorry for the boy. It reminded him of how he'd felt sorry for Jean after a low-life attacked her in her own apartment, some time ago. He'd heard her scream and pounded on her door, before rushing back to his own apartment across the hall. He had scared the attacker away as he'd hoped, but precious moments had passed while he waited behind his door, cowering, and listening for the attacker to leave. Only after the intruder had fled did he run back to her apartment where he found her, brutally beaten and as helpless as a baby. She'd been eternally grateful for what he'd done and had never expected him to confront her attacker, but secretly, he'd always wished, despite his age, that he'd had the courage to do so. Now, he stiffened his spine, trotted over to the boy, and extended his hand to him.

Cosgrove, however, hadn't finished venting and didn't appreciate Koblentz's gesture. "You want some of this, old man?"

"I was just –"

Cosgrove interrupted him with a vicious slap to the mouth that drew blood. Koblentz fell to one knee, head bowed, and was silent.

"You bastard!" Jean yelled. She glanced at Rico, who was still in his car in front of her some ten yards away. She wasn't sure how much he'd seen because his expression, as usual, was utterly inscrutable behind his aviators. She sprinted to Koblentz's side and knelt beside him. "Are you okay?"

Cosgrove glared at her, then a cruel smile lifted his mouth. She was a mouth-wateringly gorgeous woman and his mouth watered. Taunting her, he pressed one foot against Koblentz's back and slowly forced him to the ground. Jean's eyes flashed and she straightened up and slapped him hard enough to make his head turn. At once surprised and enraged, he immediately drew his arm back to retaliate. Jean closed her eyes and flinched in anticipation. Cosgrove reached far behind him to increase the momentum of his blow and then he launched his open hand toward her as hard as he could, creating a swoosh of air as his hand traveled forward to meet Jean's face.

But it never reached its target.

Rico had appeared seemingly out of nowhere and, with one hand, had grabbed Cosgrove's wrist from behind, stopping his hand mere inches from Jean's face. Now he stood behind Cosgrove, holding his wrist in a vice-like grip from which there was no hope of escape. Slender and soft, Cosgrove was around five feet ten inches tall and weighed about one hundred and seventy-five pounds. Rico stood six feet two, weighed over two hundred pounds, and was solid muscle.

He was a killer, but not your run-of-the mill killer. He was exceptional at what he did, but he was not only that. He was also a killer with a conscience. He didn't kill kids, he killed women only as a last resort, and he only killed people who "had it coming." Or at least that was what he told himself, because sometimes it was a close call. But at least he tried. And that made him unique, as nobody else in his business gave a hit a second thought.

Cosgrove tried to turn to face him, but with just one hand holding his wrist, Rico prevented him from even budging. After Cosgrove stopped squirming, Rico twisted the man's arm behind his back and wrenched it upward until he yelped in pain. Then he thrust his free forearm under Cosgrove's chin and applied just enough pressure so that Cosgrove, with some effort, could still breathe and talk. Just.

Cosgrove squealed, "What the –"

"Shut up," Rico said, and turned to Jean who was helping Koblentz to his feet. "You all right?"

"Fine." Her worried eyes met Koblentz's. She smiled. "Are you okay?"

Gingerly wiping the blood from his face, he nodded and smiled back.

"Wait in the car," Rico said.

"What are you gonna do with him?" Jean asked, a little apprehensively.

"Wait in the car."

Jean started to press him but by now she knew the drill. She collected her shopping cart and she and Koblentz headed for the car. The boy, still on his back resting on his elbows, scrambled to his feet and stood staring at Rico in awe. Rico said, "Kid, get outta here." Dejected, the boy slowly started to walk away. Raising his voice an octave, Rico said to the other gawkers, "That goes for everybody else, too."

The edge in his voice did the trick. No one objected and no one lingered. Except the boy. He turned around after he'd taken a few steps and, in a voice just above a whisper, said, "Thanks, mister."

The slightest hint of a smile appeared on Rico's face. "Nice catch, kid." That brought a grin to the boy's face. He pounded the ball in his glove and hurried away.

Rico scanned the area in a 360-degree arc and, seeing no one besides the steadily retreating onlookers, released the choke hold on Cosgrove's neck but maintained his grip on his wrist. Then he placed his free hand on the back of Cosgrove's neck and, mimicking what Cosgrove had done to Koblentz moments earlier, he slowly guided him to the ground, face down. Rico knelt beside him.

Cosgrove coughed and drew in several sweet breaths of air now that the pressure on his windpipe had been relieved. "Your ass is mine, motherfucker," he hissed under his breath.

"I don't think so," Rico said as he patted Cosgrove down. "I'm pretty attached to it."

The pat-down yielded a Smith and Wesson Model 10 .38 revolver in Cosgrove's belt under his jacket. Searching him had been a basic precaution, yet Rico hadn't expected to find a gun and when he did, he immediately regretted leaving his own in his apartment.

"Shit," he said out loud, but it was in the same tone of voice he might have used if he'd walked down three flights of stairs only to find that he'd left his cell phone upstairs in his apartment. In other words, he was irritated but not alarmed – yet. After all, this was only one guy with a .38 – no, one guy who *used to have* a .38. And so far, there was no evidence that he had company.

But there was no evidence that he was alone, either.

Rico tucked the gun in his own belt next to his belly, and with his free hand he reached down and turned Cosgrove's face toward him. He had a question. He knew he couldn't trust Cosgrove's answer but the inflexion in his voice might give him a clue. "You alone, smart ass?"

Cosgrove said nothing.

Rico increased the upward pressure on Cosgrove's arm which was still pinned behind his back. Cosgrove gritted his teeth. Rico increased the pressure again until Cosgrove could stand it no longer. He yelled, "Help!"

Maybe it was just a primal cry to the heavens, but Rico thought it was directed toward someone. Maybe more than one person. Who knew? He relaxed the pressure on Cosgrove's arm but continued to hold his wrist in a vice-like grip. With his other hand he checked the .38, engaging the cylinder release, snapping the cylinder free, spinning it with his thumb, then snapping it back in place. It was fully loaded. Six rounds. A picture of his Sig Sauer with its twelve-round capacity magazine flashed across his mind. *'This will have to do.'*

Rico looked around. Out of the corner of his eye, he saw a man rapidly advancing toward him and leveling a sawed-off shotgun in his direction. *'Must have been waiting in a car in the parking lot.'* Then he saw another man coming toward him, and another, both pointing .45's at him. *'Two more – at least.'* As they advanced, they spread out, the two men with handguns flanking him on either side and the man wielding the sawed-off shotgun directly in front of him.

The men were proceeding down a lane approximately twenty feet wide with parked cars to their left and right. The lines of parked cars ended some fifty feet in front of the spot where Rico and Cosgrove were. There were no parked cars to Rico's right or left, only open space, and the street the outfielder had crossed minutes earlier lay some thirty feet behind him. In short, running for cover was not an option. The three men had cover in the form of parked cars to their left and right. Rico had none.

He eyed the man with the shotgun. *'He can do the most damage, but he has to get closer than the other two to hit anything.'* Rico decided he would save him for last.

That left the remaining two. *'Which would be first? The tougher shot.'* His motto was: all things being equal, tackle the hardest job first. That way, whatever is left will always be easier and, therefore, relatively speaking, something to look forward to. The tougher shot would be the gunman on his left. He planned to wait until the last possible moment to start shooting so that neither of the three would know which of them was his first target until it was too late for either of the remaining two to do much about it. That meant he couldn't turn his body toward the shooter on his left ahead of time. So, with minimal time to aim, he would have to shoot across his body while kneeling beside Cosgrove, almost like a quarterback running to his right and passing to his left. A tough pass and a tougher shot. He waited.

Once Rico fired the first shot, the other two men would react in a split second, two at most. During that time each would have a decision to make. Rico figured they would have at least three choices: immediately return fire from a standing or crouching position; fall to the ground and then start firing; or take cover behind a car and open fire from there. Whatever each man did, he would have to aim first, which would consume at least an additional second tacked on to reaction time. That analysis gave Rico a minimum of two seconds to wheel around, take aim, and nail the shooter to his right – whether he was standing, crouching, lying down, or racing for cover – and then quickly take out the man with the shotgun before he inched close enough to hit anything.

The success of this plan, devised by Rico in less than three seconds, depended on everything going right, but a lot could go wrong, too. To start with, the man on the right might make it to a parked car and take cover behind it before Rico could get a shot off. If he moved quickly enough, he might just have enough time. Rico wasn't worried about the man in the middle, though. Whether he ran to his left or right, he would have to cover too much ground. And Rico was simply too fast for him to make it to either side. Of course, maybe neither man would run for cover, and maybe either or both might have faster reflexes than Rico thought.

There was a lot more that could go wrong. But that was all Rico had time to think about.

As the three gunmen continued their approach toward him, he searched their eyes for a sign. They were all cold and unyielding. Not encouraging, but Rico had something in mind that was worth a try.

"Hold it!" Rico yelled. "You wanna talk about this before somebody gets hurt?"

The men stopped in their tracks, uncertain of their next move.

Rashly, Cosgrove yelled, "Hell no!"

Instantly, the men resumed their march, now at a brisk pace. The man on Rico's left unknowingly cooperated with Rico's plan. He knelt and took aim. Rico fired a shot at him just as he'd planned, but he hadn't fired a .38 in a long time and, of course, he'd never fired this particular one. His shot went wide and grazed the left side of the man's chest. *'One thing that went wrong.'* Rico took a second to adjust his aim, but this gave the man time to fire two shots, one of which struck Rico in the thigh. *'Another thing that went wrong.'* Rico's second shot was true, though, as he adjusted for the unfamiliar gun, and passed straight through the man's heart.

The man with the shotgun, recognizing that he was out of range, began a slow trot forward. Rico ignored him. He turned to his right to sight his target, but before he could take aim, two bullets from the man's .45 slammed into his body, one piercing his chest and the other his left shoulder. *'Three things that went wrong – so far.'*

Having to fire twice at the first man had cost Rico dearly. The two bullets from the .45 had knocked him out of his kneeling position and onto his back. Meanwhile, the man, kneeling and clutching the .45 with both hands, kept shooting. Rico rolled over and, ignoring the pain and the bullets whizzing past him, propped himself up on his elbows and fired twice. The man stopped shooting. The two bullets from Rico's .38 had entered his heart.

Rico quickly scooted his body leftward and spotted the man with the shotgun, who had just slowed his trot to a walk and was leveling the shotgun toward Rico. By now Rico was thoroughly familiar with the .38 but his eyes were blurry, his arms were heavy, and his chest, thigh, and shoulder burned as though someone was stabbing him with a hot poker. He had to force all of that out of his consciousness, though, because he was out of time. The man with the shotgun closed the distance. He emptied both barrels. *'The last thing that went wrong.'* Almost simultaneously Rico squeezed off the last two rounds in the .38. Then he collapsed onto the pavement.

The man with the shotgun did, too. One bullet had entered his forehead and the other had passed through his throat.

Cosgrove, afraid to get caught in the crossfire, had lain frozen still until the shooting stopped. Now he got to his feet and pried his .38 out of Rico's hand. He pointed the gun at Rico's head and pulled the trigger. There was a "click." He pulled the trigger again and there was another "click." He had lost count. The gun was empty. He tucked it in his belt, turned his back on the bodies of his dead comrades and sprinted away.

Jean and Koblentz arrived in time to glimpse Cosgrove's back before it faded into the distance. Jean sat on the pavement and cradled Rico's head in her lap. Unable to banish the thought that somehow this was all his fault, Koblentz called 911 and then looked on helplessly.

After a moment Rico came to. Jean regarded him, a mixture of horror and sadness on her face. "Rico, Rico, please don't die."

"Who won the game?" he asked groggily.

"Oh, Rico, I wasn't listening. Please try not to talk."

"No, not that game. The one in the vacant lot across the street..."

That brought a tearful smile to her face. She glanced down at him and slowly shook her head. He met her glance and passed out.

Chapter Two

Time had flown since high school, but it didn't feel like twenty years. That's how long it had been, though, and the proof was that Paul Elliott, a successful African American lawyer, and a partner at a big firm in Chicago, was attending his twenty-year high school reunion. Seated next to him was Evelyn Rogers, an African American college math professor, whom he had met in college in Ohio. They had lost contact after graduating but years later had reunited, following the tragic deaths of their respective spouses. Now they were essentially engaged, lacking only the ring and the formal proposal.

Paul's wife had been killed by a drunk driver while she and he were jogging one evening in their Hyde Park neighborhood. A year later Evelyn's estranged husband, a heavily indebted businessman, was murdered by a hit man on orders from a mob boss from whom he had stolen a spectacularly valuable "pigeon-blood red" ruby necklace. It was a chance meeting in Honolulu that brought Paul and Evelyn together after not having seen each other since college almost fifteen years earlier. And it was in Honolulu that the hit man from Chicago had caught up with Evelyn's husband. Ironically, the same hit man, improbably, had entered Paul and Evelyn's lives a second time several months before tonight. Neither Paul nor Evelyn could have possibly forgotten him. His name was Richard Sanders, but everyone knew him as Rico.

Seated next to Paul and Evelyn were Paul's classmate Ike Johnson, a manager with a local utility company, and his wife Laura, a stay-at-home mom. Like Paul and Evelyn, both were African American, yet the couples were quite different physically. Paul was handsome in an understated way. He worked out regularly and, at around six feet two inches, had a chiseled, athletic build. Ike, by contrast, was average in appearance, shorter, balding, and slightly rotund. Evelyn, a little taller than average, was slender, yet curvaceous, and breathtakingly beautiful. Laura, a tad shorter than Ike, was comely and pleasingly plump.

Paul and Ike had seen very little of each other after graduation. Once they had brought each other up to date in a general way on their lives since then, the conversation shifted to reminiscences of other classmates. Ike, it turned out, was fixated on one classmate in particular. "I'll tell you," he mused, savoring the thought, "She was one *fine lady.*"

"Ike!" Laura, scolded, only half-jokingly.

"But seriously," he continued, "Everybody – I mean every male – was hot on her trail. And some of the teachers, too, right, Paul?"

Paul, much more reserved than Ike, would have preferred that they change the subject. He adjusted his tie and shifted positions in his chair. "Quite a few were, I guess," he conceded.

"You guess?" Ike said. "No guess about it, man. And I don't mind telling you I was one of them." He grinned mischievously and added, "What about you, Paul?"

Taken aback, Paul said weakly, "Me?"

"Anybody else sitting in that chair named Paul?" Ike retorted.

A little embarrassed, Paul glanced quickly at Evelyn who was smiling demurely, apparently amused by Ike's antics. "No, I did *not* have a crush on her," Paul said stiffly.

"Ike, quit it! Laura said, exasperated.

"What?" Ike said in the manner of a boy caught with his hand in the cookie jar and yet steadily denying it. "Paul knows I'm just pulling his chain. Right, Paul?"

Paul started to shift in his seat again, but he didn't get a chance to answer.

"Is she here?" Evelyn asked, to everyone's surprise.

"As large as life," Ike said, grinning.

"I've never seen her before, but I bet I can point her out," Evelyn said, indulging Ike.

"I'll take some of that," Ike said eagerly.

Giving up, Laura just sighed and shook her head.

Evelyn slowly scanned the room until her eyes came to rest on a group of five people – one woman and four men – engaged in a lively conversation. "That's her – over there – in the yellow skirt," she said, pointing to the woman.

"Damn, you're good," Ike said, barely containing his glee.

"Not bad," Laura conceded.

Impressed, Paul asked, "How did you know?"

"She has an air about her," Evelyn said simply.

"And four men," Ike said.

"That, too," Evelyn said. "Do you see how she's holding court?"

Paul was silent for a moment. He still wanted to change the subject, now perhaps more than before, but this time he did something about it. He stood and said to Evelyn, "Let's dance." Surprised, she rose, said, "Excuse us," to Ike and Laura, and followed him to the dance floor.

After they'd danced a few seconds in silence, Paul said, "That was very good."

"Not really," Evelyn said lightly. "I saw your reaction when she walked by earlier." Then she gave him a knowing look. If his brown skin could have turned beet red, it would have.

"Okay, you got me," he conceded sheepishly. "I did have a tiny crush on her, but like Ike said, who didn't?"

Evelyn understood. "You don't have to explain," she said gently. "I had a crush or two in high school myself."

"No!" Paul said, feigning disbelief. That brought a smile to Evelyn's face. "I just didn't see any point in confessing it to Ike, with his big mouth," he continued. "Besides, that was a long time ago." He paused for a moment. "Look, maybe I did stare a little," he said. "I didn't know it was that obvious."

"Methinks thou doth protest too much."

"On reflection, methinks so, too."

"Listen," Evelyn said after a moment. "Why don't you get it out of your system? Go over and say hello."

"It's not that big a deal."

"Paul …"

"Okay, okay. I'll go."

After their dance, Evelyn returned to their table and Paul advanced cautiously toward the alluring African American woman Evelyn had pointed out. Surrounded by her four admirers, she had an exceptionally attractive face and wore a clingy yellow skirt that displayed her curvy, well-proportioned figure. Stopping just outside her circle of admirers, Paul maneuvered around until he was standing in front of her. When her eyes finally met his, he said, "Excuse me. Aren't you Valerie – is it still Wallace?"

She took a few steps in his direction. "I'm Valerie, but it's now Bennett. You're Paul …"

"Elliott," he said.

Valerie glanced at her four cohorts. "I'm sorry. You all remember Paul Elliott, don't you?"

Each of the four then gave him an obligatory nod and awkwardly shook hands with him as they introduced themselves.

Intrigued, Valerie said, "Will you gentlemen excuse us, please? We'll just be a few minutes."

Disappointed, each of the four silently excused himself and reluctantly drifted away.

When Evelyn returned to the table, Ike rose quickly and held her chair for her as she sat. "I hope I didn't put my foot in my mouth," he said, chastened.

"You didn't put it in because you never take it out," Laura said.

Ike frowned.

"Oh, it's nothing," Evelyn said. "I suggested he go over and say hello."

"Whew!" Ike said, making an exaggerated imitation of wiping sweat from his brow. "That was close."

They all laughed.

Valerie, chatting with Paul, glanced over and saw Evelyn laughing with Ike and Laura. "Evelyn... Such a pretty name for such a pretty girl. Actually, she's very beautiful. You did well for yourself."

"*I* think so."

"Would you like to dance? Evelyn won't mind, will she?"

It was a slow dance and Paul hesitated. "Well..."

"Good," she said, taking his hand and leading him to the dance floor. "I didn't think so."

As they reached the dance floor, Paul said, "So you're in sales, huh?"

"I was always good with people. You probably remember."

"But not from personal experience."

"Naughty Paul."

"No, I just meant..."

"That's okay," she said. After a pause, she continued. "Do you remember Joe Bennett?"

"He's your husband?"

"Yes, but do you remember him?"

"No, should I?"

"Not really. Most of the people in our class don't. I barely remember him myself and I married him." Her mouth twitched.

"Nice guy?"

"He is. But a girl should have a better reason than that to marry a man."

There followed a moment of silence. For Paul it was an awkward one. For Valerie it was not. "So, you're very successful," she said. "I could tell you would be."

"Oh?"

"Yes. You had that look."

"Really?"

"Yes, really."

There followed another moment of silence, this time broken by Paul. "You know, I had a crush on you," he said abruptly. "Did you have any idea?"

She wasn't surprised. "I guess so. I thought you were cute and all but ... Tell me – why didn't you ever do anything about it?"

"Would it have made any difference if I had?"

"I guess we'll never know," she said.

"I had a lot of competition back then."

"You still do."

Paul raised an eyebrow and started to say something, but Valerie noticed his reaction and spoke first. "Don't get excited," she teased. "I'm a happily married woman, remember?"

Chapter Three

It was still a beautiful day for a ball game, and the sun still shone brightly when the ambulance arrived to transport Rico to a nearby hospital. It had taken four minutes after the 911 operator dispatched it, and nine minutes later the attendants wheeled Rico into the Emergency Room of Advocate Trinity Hospital.

He had been right about the range of the shotgun. Although the man wielding it had managed to empty both barrels before Rico dropped him, none of the buckshot found its mark. Instead, the blasts only kicked up swirls of dust and gravel close enough to Rico that he felt the sting of a slew of stones and specks of gravel against his legs, but nothing broke the skin. Therefore, the doctors only had to contend with the injuries which just two of the three shooters had inflicted: wounds to the chest, right thigh, and left shoulder. The bullet to the chest from the .45 had shattered a rib and left a nasty, gaping hole. But while it had missed his heart – barely – and his lungs and major blood vessels, it had struck one of the smaller arteries, causing internal bleeding which had to be repaired and monitored. The wounds to the shoulder and thigh, while grave, were not life-threatening.

When Rico regained consciousness, his first vision was that of Jean asleep, curled up in a chair in the corner of the room, her flame-red hair fanned out across a white pillow. He tried in vain to get up and found himself hooked up to an IV and a heart monitor, and discovered that his left shoulder, torso, and right leg were heavily bandaged. He surveyed his injuries, groaned, and said, "Shit." He flopped his head back onto the stiff white hospital pillow.

Jean awakened and stretched. "How do you feel?" she murmured, her voice thick with exhaustion.

"How long have I been here?"

Jean ambled over to his bed and sat next to him. "About three days. Now how about answering *my* question?"

"Which was?"

"How do you feel?"

"Lousy."

"For a while they didn't think you were going to make it. I was worried to death."

"When can I get outta here?"

"Glad to see you, too." Her lips quirked up into a smile.

"You been here the whole time?"

"Mostly, yeah."

"Well..."

"Yes?"

"Thanks for stayin'. You didn't have to, you know."

"Sure, I did."

"Did you now?"

Jean scooted closer to him and took his hand in hers. "Yes. And if I were lying here, you would be here for me, too."

"Don't be so sure."

She sighed. "Okay, Mr. Tough Guy. I'm glad you're all right."

"That makes two of us," Rico said. He grimaced as a sharp pain shot through his chest. "What the hell happened, anyway? I remember patting the guy down and finding his piece. Then the lights went out."

"What happened was he had three buddies."

"Jesus."

"Somehow you managed to kill all three," Jean said and in a mildly sarcastic tone she added, "You should be proud of yourself."

"I am," Rico said. "I'm still alive – barely."

"I'm sorry. I didn't mean it the way it came out. Only ..."

"I know. Don't sweat it. Just tell me, what happened to the other guy?"

"Gone," Jean said. "The cops are looking but they don't even know who he is."

"Shit," Rico said. Restless and frustrated, he tried to sit up a little and again winced in pain and gave up. It felt like someone was driving a stake through his chest.

Jean stood and adjusted the angle of the bed for him. "You're using that word a lot today. What's the matter?"

"Nothing. Just thinkin'."

"No, there's something else."

His features hardened. "I was just thinkin'... I'd like to get my hands on him."

Jean started to protest. "Rico –"

But he changed the subject. "What did the cops say?"

"They just wanna talk. They know it was self-defense."

"Christ. It was probably all over the news, too."

"What did you expect?"

Rico just shook his head, took in a lung-full of air, and slowly blew it out through his mouth.

"You think he might come here?" Jean asked.

"Who?"

"You know who."

"No. He probably blew town by now."

"You aren't just saying that?"

A worried, anxious look etched on her face, Jean sat on the bed again, this time very close to him.

"No. Three days, you said? If he was thinkin' about that, he woulda been here by now."

"And what about you?"

"What about me?"

"You said you'd like to get your hands on him."

"I would. But what am I gonna do from this hospital bed?"

She persisted. "And after you get out?"

"Jean, you're a helluva lady, but let's not do this dance right now, okay?" As soon as he said it, he thought better of it. "Listen," he added, "If he wants to walk away from this, maybe we can call it even. I took out – what? – three of his guys? – and I'm still here. Does that make you happy?"

"If you really mean it, yes."

"I'm not lookin' to start World War III if I don't have to. So, I mean it. Now be happy."

"I am," she said, seemingly satisfied, and leaned in and gave him a peck on the cheek.

"Good," Rico said. "Now do me a favor."

"Anything."

"Bring me my piece – just in case."

Jean left the hospital and returned within the hour with Rico's Sig Sauer, a handkerchief, and a roll of gray plumber's tape. They covered the gun with the handkerchief so that the tape wouldn't stick to it and then they secured the .45 to the metal rail on the underside of his bed, in reach of his right hand when he dangled his arm over the side of the bed. Now he could rest easy.

Chapter Four

The next day Jean arose earlier than usual, around seven, showered and dressed in a conservative black skirt with a hem just below the knee and matching jacket, along with a white blouse and black heels. She wore her hair up in an elegant twist and she applied minimal makeup. She had a light breakfast of toast and coffee and took the bus downtown. For all appearances, she was just another one of the thousands of office workers who made the same journey that day from various parts of the city and suburbs.

She got off on LaSalle Street and made her way to one of the many venerable office buildings standing shoulder to shoulder lining both sides of the street. It was another impeccably beautiful day without a cloud in the sky, but you would never know it standing anywhere on this section of LaSalle, because the towering buildings blotted out the morning sun. Jean mentally confirmed the address and entered the massive lobby occupied by multiple elevator banks. Initially overwhelmed, she spied the building directory on the wall almost immediately in front of her. She strolled over and quickly found the name she was looking for. Then she located the appropriate elevator bank and after a brief wait, got on with several other passengers and took the elevator to the thirty-second floor. She and another woman got off, along with a man she hadn't noticed, who got off last. She hadn't noticed him either when he got on her bus right after she did that morning, or when he got off immediately after she did on LaSalle Street, or when he had followed her into the building and onto the elevator.

The elevator opened onto a reception area that oozed power, prestige, and old money. The mahogany paneled walls were adorned with photographs of long-deceased founding partners of the firm. The other woman, who obviously worked there, entered the reception area first and, without stopping, said good morning to the receptionist seated at the desk in front of her, turned right, and proceeded down a long hall that was perpendicular to the desk. The receptionist greeted the woman and then, smiling brightly, turned to Jean, who was now standing in front of the reception desk.

"Good morning. How may I help you?" she asked.

"Good morning. I'd like to see Mr. Paul Elliott."

"Your name, please?"

"Jean Webber. But I don't have an appointment."

"I see," the receptionist said rather dubiously. "Well, please have a seat and I'll see whether he's available."

Jean took a seat in one of the many plush armchairs situated behind the receptionist desk, as the receptionist greeted the man who, unbeknownst to Jean, had been following her all morning.

"How may I help you, sir?"

"I'm sorry," he said. "I think I got off on the wrong floor."

Before the receptionist could offer her assistance, the man turned and walked briskly back to the elevator.

The receptionist raised an eyebrow but then promptly forgot about the man and called Paul and told him about Jean.

"I don't recognize the name," he said. "Did she say anything else?"

"No. If you'd like I can ask her the reason for her visit."

"That won't be necessary. I have a few minutes. Is there a conference room available?"

"Sure. You can take the Lake Room."

"Good. I'm on my way."

Paul hoped this wasn't a sales pitch of some kind. If so, he was sure it wouldn't take more than a few minutes to listen politely and send

Ms. Webber on her way. Fortunately, his calendar was pretty clear that morning.

When he reached the reception desk, there was another woman seated on the other side of the room across from Jean waiting to see another lawyer, and the receptionist pointed Jean out to Paul with a practiced nod of her head. He gazed at her and creased his brow. In front of him sat a spectacularly beautiful woman with striking red hair, but he had no idea who she was. He strolled over to where she sat.

"Ms. Webber?"

She stood. "Yes."

He extended his hand. "Paul Elliott."

Shaking his hand, she said, "How do you do, Mr. Elliott. But please call me Jean."

"All right, Jean. I'm sorry, I don't remember, but have we met?"

"No, I'm a friend of a friend…Well, maybe not exactly a friend. A mutual acquaintance, Richard Sanders."

That didn't ring a bell. "I'm afraid I don't –"

"Can we talk in private?"

Paul hesitated. He didn't know anybody named Richard Sanders. '*This might be the perfect time to cut this meeting short.*' Unsure what he was going to say next, he glanced at his watch and then back at her. Her eyes pleaded with him.

"I know you're busy," she said.

'*Not really,*' Paul thought.

"But it'll just take a few minutes," she said. "I promise."

'*I guess I can spare a few minutes,*' he thought. And he was curious about who Richard Sanders was. "Sure," he said at last. "Come with me."

They headed down the hall toward the conference room. On the way they encountered another lawyer from the firm, accompanied by a young boy of about twelve or thirteen coming from the opposite direction. As the four approached each other, the two lawyers silently greeted each other with a nod, but when the boy saw Jean, his eyes widened, and his jaw dropped. He'd recognized her but she hadn't recognized him. She was used to that kind of admiring reaction but was, nevertheless, secretly flattered by what she assumed was the boy's innocent response to seeing a pretty lady, and she acknowledged him with a kind smile.

Once past Jean, the boy turned his head and stared at her over his shoulder. While Jean was an exceptionally attractive woman, the lawyer accompanying the boy was surprised that he was old enough to notice. Marveling at his excellent taste in women, he placed an arm around the boy's shoulder and hurried him along.

When they reached the tasteful conference room, Paul showed Jean to a chair at an ornate, golden brown conference table fashioned from Bocote, an exotic wood native to Mexico, Central America, and the West Indies, that spanned almost the length of the room. Taking a seat across from her, he said, "Now tell me about Richard Sanders."

"You remember a while ago when you and your girlfriend Evelyn ..."

"Rogers."

"When you and she had some trouble with a man named Frank Wilson...?"

When Paul heard the name, he scooted to the edge of his chair. "Go on."

"And then you had a run-in last year with John D'Angelo. I found out about both from Richard Sanders."

Paul stood, lost in thought, and paced back and forth a few steps. "Richard Sanders... So that's his name."

"You probably know him as Rico," Jean said.

"Rico?"

"Yeah. That's what everybody calls him."

"I know who you're talking about," Paul said. "But believe it or not, this is the first time I've heard his name – either one of them."

Jean had been holding it together all morning, but now she started to become emotional. Her voice cracking, she said, "It figures. He saves your life and he doesn't even tell you his name."

She began to cry softly, and Paul offered her a tissue from a box resting on a nearby credenza. "I didn't mean to upset you," he said.

Jean wiped her eyes. "I'm sorry. I don't usually…"

"It's okay."

After a moment she composed herself. "He was shot four days ago, and he almost didn't make it. He was just trying to protect me from a lousy creep…"

"Of course," Paul said. "Richard Sanders. That's the name that was in the paper."

"Then you should understand. The animal who started it all is still out there, and I been around long enough to know these creeps always know somebody who wants to get even. If he wasn't so helpless right now…"

"Isn't he safe in the hos –"

"What?"

"I started to say "hospital" but maybe not. Wouldn't the police –"

"You know as well as I do that the cops aren't gonna lift a finger to help a guy like Rico," Jean said. "But that's not the problem. He's getting out soon."

"So, what would you like me to do?" Paul asked.

"Nothing illegal. I just want you to help me find a place to hide him until he's strong enough to protect himself. Any place I could hide him out they would know about or be able to find, but no one would ever suspect you."

Paul frowned, returned to his chair, and sat facing Jean. "I know it doesn't seem like it to you, but it's not that easy."

"Because it's bringing back some things you'd rather forget?"

"That's part of it."

"Like you taking out some low life who had it coming?"

Paul propped his elbows up on the table and leaned in closer to Jean. "You mentioned my girlfriend Evelyn a minute ago," Paul said. "I thought the man I killed was trying to kill her."

"And because he was really trying to kill Rico, that makes it so terrible?" Jean said.

"No. It would be terrible either way."

"From where I sit, it would've been more terrible if Rico had got it instead. But you saved his life, even if you didn't mean to. And he's paid you back two times over."

"I never asked for his help," Paul said defensively.

"And he didn't ask for yours either," Jean said, her voice rising. "But he got it anyway and you got his. Now you're both alive. And you know what? He's still not asking. But I am."

"My compliments. You argue a pretty good case. But it's just not that simple."

"What is? Listen, we both know that Rico's no saint. I can't change him; I've tried. God knows I've tried. He is what he is – even if he's not your kind of people."

"Wait a minute," Paul said. "I never said –"

"I know you didn't. But let's face it." She stood and meandered over to the side of the room. Looking around and surveying it from floor to ceiling, she said, "Him and me – we're both out of place in a joint like this."

"I know what you mean."

"You do?"

"Yes. I felt pretty much the same way when I started here, way back when."

Paul had been the first black lawyer hired by his law firm and seven years later, its first black partner. He had come from modest circumstances – his father had been an auto mechanic and his mother a nurse – and it took a while for him to get used to the rarified atmosphere of Big Firm practice. Fortunately, he had had good mentors.

"Then I guess we got something in common – you, me, and Rico," Jean said.

"I guess you could say so."

"You wanna know something?" Jean said. "He would never admit it but for some reason he likes you. And he doesn't like many people. So even if you told me to take a hike – I mean if he found out about it – he would save your life again if it came to that."

Paul stood and faced her. "Jean –"

But she wasn't finished. "I think he sees something in you," she said, glancing around again. "I mean, besides all this. Like I see something in him. Maybe you can see something in him, too, if you try."

Paul sighed deeply. He needed to say something he had intended to keep to himself, but then maybe she already knew. "This is why it's not so simple. Did he ever say anything to you about Honolulu?"

"No, but I know a couple of people died while he was over there."

"One of them was Evelyn's husband. Soon to be ex, but still …"

"I get it now," Jean said, dejected.

"There's more," Paul said. "He thought Evelyn and I had a valuable piece of jewelry he was trying to get back. We didn't have it, but he came very close to killing us before he found out Evelyn's husband actually had it." Paul paused a moment. "I'm over it. He did save our lives later and likely mine again – after I inadvertently saved his. But Evelyn can't quite bring herself to…"

"Forgive him?"

Paul nodded.

"I can see how that would be hard. You really care about her, huh?"

Paul nodded again.

"Well, I guess that's that," Jean said. "Thanks for listening anyway." She turned and started for the door.

Paul heaved another great sigh. "Hold on."

Jean stopped and turned to face him. Her eyes brightened.

"No promises but let me see what I can do," he said wearily. He paused for a second then added, "And I didn't mean what I said a minute ago about never asking for his help."

A broad smile on her face, Jean rushed toward him, arms outstretched as if to embrace him, but she caught herself and stopped just short of where he was standing. "That Rico," she said, beaming. "He's a real perspicacious guy."

Paul smiled. "Perspicacious? That's a pretty fancy word."

"Yeah. He just uses it with me."

"I see," Paul said, curious. "So how is he perspicacious?"

"Remember I said I thought he sees something in you? Well, it looks like maybe he was right."

Paul said nothing.

"I need to ask you one more thing," she said. "A minute ago, you said he probably saved your life a second time. You knew about that?"

"Yes."

"You knew he didn't want you to find out?"

"Yes."

"I guess he's not the only one who's perspicacious."

Later that morning Larry Cosgrove paid a visit to his uncle, Gus Chakiras, a local mobster who ran things in the neighborhood. He was world-weary, short, balding, and in his mid-sixties. It was understood that before anybody took out anybody else in the neighborhood, Gus's approval was necessary, and if anybody in the neighborhood pulled a job there or anywhere else, Gus received a percentage of the take, which was his "tribute" so to speak. He paid off the policemen who patrolled the area and some of the aldermen and judges, and these payments provided protection for most of the criminals in the neighborhood, from small time hustlers to contract killers, so long as they paid regular tribute to Gus and did as they were told.

Rico lived on the periphery of the neighborhood. Although an argument could be made that he actually operated within Gus's territory, at least occasionally, whether he did or didn't was irrelevant, because he was a free-lancer, in the neighborhood and anywhere else he worked. He did jobs for Gus and other Chicago bosses, but he paid tribute to no one. He didn't have to. Other guys needed a boss's protection. Rico didn't. And none of the bosses wanted to try to force their protection on him, because, first of all, success would have been an uncertain proposition. Secondly, they needed his services more than they needed trouble with him, because he was better at what he did than anyone else they could find.

Being a free-lancer, though, meant that if he got himself into a jam, he had to get himself out of it. Which was okay with him. In fact, that's the way he preferred it. He lived like a monk and over the years, he'd always put money aside and seldom had to dip into his sizeable reserves. Some he kept in cash in a safety deposit box, some he kept in a checking account, and some he kept in a brokerage account. Over the years he'd never had to make bail, but if he'd had to, he wouldn't have needed to call Gus or anyone else. He could've paid the freight himself. He'd never needed a criminal lawyer, because he'd never been arrested, but if he ever did, he was pretty sure he'd be able to afford a good one.

This business with Rico was a hot potato for Gus. The public shootout was inexcusable. It never should have happened, and normally he would have had the hide of the hothead who'd blundered into it. Unfortunately, though, the hothead was his nephew, the son of his favorite sister, and he had to tread lightly.

Although Rico was a free-lancer, coming and going as he pleased and doing jobs for bosses like Gus, when it suited him, technically – at least where business was concerned – Gus still called the shots and he was due a certain amount of deference and even respect. But this dust-up with Larry wasn't business. It was personal. And Gus knew that.

Gus's nephew had tried to kill Rico because of something which had nothing to do with business, and the way Rico saw it, he was doing Gus a favor by negotiating with him. Technically, Frank Wilson had also called the shots where business was concerned, and he too had been due a certain amount of deference and even respect – until Rico killed him. That had also been personal. And Gus knew that, too.

On Gus's orders, Larry had reluctantly lain low for the past few days, waiting to see whether Rico would live or die. If he died, problem solved. But because he'd survived, he had to be dealt with.

Gus summoned Larry to his home to discuss how to deal with Rico going forward. The two men sat at a picnic table in Gus's back yard. Larry was being just as hardheaded as he was impulsive.

"I'm tellin' you like I did when they first wheeled him into the hospital," Gus said, "This is somebody you don't wanna fuck with, kid."

"And I'm tellin' you I didn't start this, Gus. He did."

"Says you."

"He stuck his nose in."

"After you got into it with some kid."

"I don't care. I'm not walkin' away."

Gus glared at him. "You can walk away or be carried away. Take your choice."

"Yeah, well, right now he's flat on his back in that hospital. I could just waltz in there and blow his fuckin' brains out."

"So, what are you doin' hangin' around here then?" Larry started to get up, raring to go, like a bull waiting to be released from a shoot at a rodeo. Gus stopped him with a hand on his shoulder. "I already know what you got down here," he said, pointing to his crotch. "I wanna know what you got up here," Gus said, placing an index finger on his temple. "If you give him an inch, this guy will eat you for breakfast. So, you're thinkin' he's laid up right now and maybe he don't got that inch. So now is a good time. Larry, maybe three days ago – or even two – was a good time. But not today. Today the man is conscious and there ain't no more good times."

Larry sneered. "He's not that good."

"Come here," Gus said.

"What for?"

"Just come here."

Larry walked around the table and stood in front of Gus. "What?"

Gus rose abruptly and before Larry could react, he slapped him twice in quick succession, once with his palm and then again with the back of his hand. Larry took an instinctive half-step forward but there was no chance he would retaliate, or even complain. He took the slaps without a word. Gus stared into Larry's eyes for a full thirty seconds, daring him to retaliate. Finally, Larry blinked. Gus sat and with a wave of his hand commanded Larry to sit, too.

"He's not that good, you say? You think your three buddies would back you up on that – I mean, if they could talk?"

Larry rolled his eyes skyward, deep skepticism registering on his face.

"You haven't heard a word I've said, have you?" Gus growled. "Six shots and three dumb-asses dead."

"And if I'd had just one more round ..."

"If, if. 'If' never built shit."

"I'm not afraid of him, Gus."

"I know you're not, but you should be."

Seemingly defeated, Larry stood and folded his arms across his chest. "So, what do you want me to do?"

"Develop a case of amnesia and hope I can convince him to do the same."

"And what about Cleveland? Is he gonna get amnesia, too?"

"You just worry about Larry. Let me worry about Cleveland."

Chapter Five

Rico lay wide awake as one of his doctors stood next to his bed examining his chart. The IV and heart monitor were gone but the heavy bandages on his left shoulder, torso, and right leg remained.

"Even with your extensive injuries, I could tell by your muscle tone that you were in excellent physical condition," the doctor said. "However, I never imagined that you would make such a rapid recovery. As a matter of fact, I'm astonished."

"Does that mean I can get outta here soon?"

"Yes, any time now. Mostly you need rest and you can get that at home. You do have someone who can help look after you for a while, don't you?"

"Sure," Rico said, not meaning it. "I got that covered."

The doctor glanced at Rico's chart again. "I see you don't smoke, and you only drink socially. Tell me, what do you do to stay in such good shape?"

"Nothing special," Rico said. "Push-ups, sit-ups, weights, and jogging. Not too much of anything. Just enough to make it hurt."

"Well, keep it up," the doctor said. "That is, once you're back to your old self, which shouldn't be too long based on your progress so far. The nurse will go over your homegoing instructions with you before you're discharged, and she'll let you know when you can gradually resume your exercise routine." He extended his hand to Rico. "Good luck if I don't see you before you're discharged."

Rico shook his hand. "Thanks. I was pretty lucky already. I don't think I'll need any more."

"There's one more thing," the doctor said. "There's a detective outside in the hall. I asked him to wait until I examined you. I trust this won't be too upsetting after everything you've already gone through. As you know, I'm not a psychologist, but emotionally, you seem fine to me. How do you feel about talking to him now?"

"You mean I have a choice?"

"If you'd rather he come back some other time, I can ask him to do that."

Rico smiled. "Just kidding, doc. Send him in."

"Good luck again," the doctor said and left the room.

Thirty seconds later the detective came in. He was short and portly – at least fifteen pounds overweight – and he was in his mid-fifties. Rico eyed him from head to toe as he entered the room. His wing-tipped shoes were freshly shined, and his suit appeared to be newly dry cleaned. He walked with a barely perceptible limp, and Rico wondered whether it was the result of a gunshot wound and whether he might suffer the same fate.

As he approached Rico's bed, he removed his badge and held it out in front of him. "Mr. Sanders, my name is Lieutenant Cannon. Your doctor tells me it's okay if I ask you a few questions."

"Go right ahead."

"Mind if I sit?" he asked, while taking out a note pad and pen and sliding a chair from the corner of the room over to Rico's bedside.

"How are you feeling?" Cannon asked as he sat down.

"I'll live."

"Well, I don't have very many questions. We've talked to several witnesses, including Ms. Webber – your girlfriend, is it?"

"You could call her that."

"I'm curious. What do you do for a living, Mr. Sanders? When we asked Ms. Webber, she said we should ask you."

"That sounds like her."

"So, what *do* you do?"

"A little of this and a little of that."

"That's a tad vague, don't you think?"

"Could be."

"Then, be more specific."

"I'm an independent contractor. I work for a lot of people."

"What exactly do you do?"

"A little of this and a little of that."

"We're going in circles. Is there some reason you don't want to answer my question?"

"You mean answer again? I already told you."

"Well, I can't force you to answer, but something tells me you already knew that."

"Yes, just like you already knew what I do for a living."

Cannon sighed and gave up, but with a smile. He knew exactly what Rico did for a living. His reputation had preceded him. Even though they had never been able to pin anything on him, all the detectives in that District – and most of the others – knew who he was. But Cannon wanted to hear it from Rico's own mouth, out of curiosity more than anything else. How would an enforcer and hit man describe what he did for a living? An independent contractor. He had his answer and since Rico had clearly acted in self-defense, he moved on.

The sole reason for his visit was to confirm for the record something else he already knew - either Rico couldn't identify Larry, or if he could, he wouldn't. "I take it you can't identify the man who caused this cluster-fuck?"

"Cluster-fuck?" Rico said wryly. "Is that a police term?"

"You know what I mean."

"No, I can't ID him. I never seen him before – or since."

"But you know how to find him, don't you?"

"Not a clue."

"Really?"

"Really."

"And I take it you don't expect him to look you up?"

"Him and what army?"

"Pretty cocky, huh?"

"I try not to be. But sometimes I can't help myself."

"Maybe you got a right. You weren't armed, were you?"

"No."

"So, you took his piece away from him and used it on the other three guys?"

"That's what they tell me."

"Where was yours?"

"I'm sure you know I got a permit. It was in my apartment."

"What kind is it?"

"Sig."

"Nice weapon."

"I think so."

Smith sighed for the second time since he began the interview and stood. "I guess that's it, unless you want to tell me who that guy is."

"Like I said, I never seen him before."

"You got anything else you want to say?"

"You take one in the leg?"

"Yeah, a while ago."

"You ever gonna get rid of that limp?"

"It's not so bad, but I don't think so. Why? You worried about yours?"

"Either way, I don't think it'll cramp my style."

Cannon turned to leave and stopped. He was curious about something. "One more thing. Why didn't you try to negotiate with the attackers?"

"Elucidate."

"The witnesses said ... Hold on a minute." He took out his notebook and flipped through it until he found the page he was searching for. "They said you 'asked the shooters whether they wanted to talk before anybody got hurt' or words to that effect."

"That sounds like negotiation to me," Rico said.

"What I mean is, you had the guy's .38. You could've threatened to shoot him if his friends didn't back off. Or you could've stood him up and used him as a shield to keep them from firing at you."

Rico rubbed his chin and thought for a moment. "Well, like I told you, there's a lot I don't remember about that day. But lookin' at it logically, the creep I was holdin' down was guilty of three things that I knew about: he knocked a young kid on his ass because the kid accidentally ran into him and ruined his day by smashin' all of his liquor bottles; he put his hands on an old man who came over to help the kid up; and he tried to put his hands on Jean after she got in his face for what he did to the kid and the old man." He paused to give Cannon a chance to react.

"Go on," Cannon said. "I'm listening."

"So, I threaten to blow this guy's head off if his pals don't back off, like you say. What if they don't back off? Chances are, they will, but what if they don't? One rule I live by is I never threaten to do somethin' I'm not prepared to do if I hafta. So, what if they don't back off and I waste this guy like I threaten to? Now, what if the three guys take off? They might or they might not. But what if they do? The cops show up and wanna know why I popped this guy with his own gun. I got three reasons I can prove: the kid, the old man, and Jean. That's not enough to beat a murder rap."

"Murder? It would have been self-defense. The three men who ran away were accomplices of the dead man and they were threatening your life," Cannon said.

"But *the dead guy* wasn't threatening my life. He was unarmed because I took his piece, and he couldn't move unless I let him. In fact, he was yellin' for help if I remember correctly."

"You had witnesses, though."

"If the State's Attorney wants to believe the witnesses, I'm golden. But what if he doesn't? The three shooters never intended to shoot anybody. They just saw me take their buddy's gun away from him and kick the shit outta him and they just showed up to try to convince me to let him go. Instead, I put a bullet in his head, and they run away, scared that I might do the same to them. What I'm sayin' is, I'm not the most popular guy in the State's Attorney's office, and if I off this guy, he can spin this thing any way he wants."

"I don't think you're giving the State's Attorney enough credit," Cannon said.

"Think what you want," Rico said. "But it would be my ass."

"And what about standing him up and using him as a shield, maybe until somebody called 911, or maybe if you agreed to let him go, they would've backed off."

"I'm six-two and the guy is, maybe, five-nine or five-ten. I stand be-hind him and maybe one of the shooters thinks he can put one through my head. Maybe he can and maybe he can't, but the point is, maybe he *thinks* he can. Then, where am I? And as for lettin' him go if they agree to back off, same thing. Maybe they really do back off, but maybe they don't. Which leaves me where? I'll tell you where. I let him go and they don't back off. That leaves me maybe dead."

Cannon heaved a great sigh. "I didn't expect all that."

"I feel like I'm playin' three-dimensional chess," Rico said.

"Did all of that really go through your mind?"

"Like I said, I don't remember everything, but if I had time, that would've been the long version."

Cannon raised an eyebrow. "And what was the short version?"

"I figure I had maybe three seconds before all hell broke loose. In that time, I thought whatever I thought. I don't remember. Some of it was probably instinct. But based on the long version I just gave you, I think I made the right decision."

"You know, you seem like a guy who could do something else with his life," Cannon said. "Why don't you?"

"Because I like what I'm doin' with my life. Besides, I'm not laid up in this hospital bed because of what I'm doin' with my life. I'm here because I was bein' a good Samaritan. You don't have anything against good Samaritans, do you, Lieutenant?"

"If you put it that way," Cannon said, "I hope your luck holds up."

Lieutenant Cannon had been gone about an hour when in the distance Rico heard footsteps approaching. Too loud for a doctor or a nurse. Both invariably wore soft soles. His hand moved to grab the .45 taped to the underside of his bed, but as the footsteps grew louder, he relaxed, exhaled deeply, and released his grip on the .45. He'd recognized the cadence of the high heels. They belonged to Jean.

"Come in," Rico said a second before she appeared in the doorway.

"Recognize my high stepping?"

"You fooled me at first. Trying to throw me off?"

"I haven't worn these heels in a while. They hurt a little. I guess that explains it."

"You have my permission to buy a new pair."

After her meeting with Paul, Jean was on cloud nine. She was so anxious to see Rico that she'd rushed straight to the hospital. She hurried over to the bed, sat beside him, and gave him a kiss. "How are you today?"

"That helps," he said, looking her over. "Who died? You look like you just came from a funeral."

"Well, at least you noticed," she teased.

"Oh, oh. Here we go," Rico said, feigning annoyance. "Okay. The outfit looks great. You look great. Now can we move on?"

"Only because you're laid up and I feel sorry for you," she teased. Then her tone turned serious. "Rico, you know they want to let you go home soon."

"So I hear. The sooner the better."

"I don't think you should be alone until – until you're stronger."

"You can stop by every once-in-a-while, but I'll be okay."

She wasn't getting through to him. She stood, moved to one side of the room, turned to face him, and folded her arms in front of her chest. "I know you will, but I still don't want you to be alone. I want to take care of you for a while, but I think we should get out of the city. You know that place outside of town you used sometimes burned down, so that's no good. I know this guy who has a cabin in the country about a hundred miles from here.... Well, I went to see him today."

"What guy?" His voice was neutral, but it carried an undertone of suspicion. He wasn't a jealous man, but he knew Jean was holding something back.

"Just a guy I know."

"A guy you know? Come on, Jean. Like I wasn't gonna ask."

She strolled back and stood next to the bed. Her voice was almost defiant. "Paul Elliott."

"You shittin' me? Jesus, Jean."

She sat on the side of the bed beside him and shrugged her shoulders. "What? You save his life and I can't ask him for a favor?"

"And if I had caught up with him and his girlfriend before this creep tried to pop me, I woulda wasted 'em both."

The truth, of course, was more complicated. He just didn't feel like explaining all of it to Jean right then and there.

"Why didn't you tell me before now?" Jean said. "I had to hear it from him."

"It was business."

"It's always 'business'."

"What do you want from me, Jean? It's what I do. It's who I am."

He tried to adjust his pillow so that he could sit up straighter but was having difficulty. Jean reached over to help. Rico grudgingly accepted her assistance.

"This was different," she continued. "This lawyer and his girlfriend – they aren't like the creeps you deal with. I've only met him, but they seem like nice people."

"Sometimes nice people get hurt."

"And that makes it all right?"

"It makes it what it is."

"You don't want to admit it, but I think you feel bad that you almost killed them."

"Think what you want."

"Rico, talk to me."

Genuinely perplexed, he shrugged. "Why did you ask him to stick his neck out for me after what he told you?"

Jean stood, turned her back to him. "You're changing the subject."

"Like hell I am. Why did you ask him?"

"Because you stuck your neck out for him and his girlfriend."

"And you think that squares it?"

She turned, faced him. "*He* thinks so."

Rico shrugged again, closed his eyes for a moment, deep in thought. He still didn't like the idea but for her sake, he could live with it. "Okay, you wore me down. I give up. Tell your friend –"

"*My* friend?"

"Yeah, *your* friend. Tell him we'll take him up on his offer. I always wanted to spend some time in the country."

That evening after work Paul planned to tell Evelyn about his meeting with Jean. It would be a difficult conversation, one he didn't look forward to having, but putting it off wasn't going to make it any easier. Once he arrived at the townhouse he and Evelyn shared, he sat her down in the den and told her he had something important say. She wanted him to come right out and say what was on his mind, rather than keeping her in suspense. Over her protestations, he poured a glass of wine for her and made himself a bourbon and water on the rocks before beginning.

At first, she thought he might have been about to propose. That would have come as a shock, a pleasant one but a shock, nonetheless. They had been living together for several months, but they had not set a wedding date, and the unspoken consensus between them was that they wouldn't rush things. So, she rapidly abandoned that thought. Moreover, his mood was somber, not what would be expected of a man who was about to propose, not even a serious and sober man like Paul. Whatever he was building up to, she decided it had to be bad news.

Paul took a healthy swig from his drink and, as precisely as he could recall, he described Jean's unannounced visit to his office, her surprising request, his initial reluctance to help, and his ultimate acquiescence. Evelyn's reaction was swift.

"Paul, this is insane," she said, rising from her chair and setting her wine glass – from which she hadn't taken a sip – on a nearby side table. "Why should he expect you to get involved in this?"

The answer was obvious, he thought, and he wondered whether in her anger, she had simply ignored whatever she didn't want to hear. "You know the answer to that," he said tersely.

"He's a murderer, Paul. What about the people he killed?"

"That would be your late, philandering husband and his girlfriend, who used to be a friend of yours," he pointed out sarcastically and immediately regretted it.

"So, they were thieves and adulterers. That doesn't mean they deserved to be murdered."

Paul stood and faced her. "Okay, that was a stupid thing to say. But the bottom line is, he saved both our lives once and likely mine a second time, although he tried to conceal it from me. I owe him this much."

"You may believe you do, but you don't – not really."

Again, the truth was complicated. For no reason other than pique and wounded pride, Frank Litvak, the mob boss who had originally paid Rico to kill Paul and Evelyn insisted on having them killed, even after they'd returned the necklace to him. When Rico declined to do the job, Litvak had threatened Jean's life. Faced with that threat, Rico, unsure what he would do, had reluctantly set out to kill them, but he was still pondering whether he would actually go through with it when, at the last minute, the decision was made for him. Through a bizarre twist of fate, Paul had saved Rico's life, and Rico had told Litvak in no uncertain terms that, henceforth, Paul and Evelyn were off limits. When Litvak disagreed, Rico had killed him and considered himself to be in Paul's debt for a lifetime, which led to Rico arguably saving Paul's life a second time, several months later.

"Well, I guess I have to be the judge of how much I owe him," Paul said, reluctantly but firmly.

Evelyn was stunned by the finality of his statement. She sat down and for a moment was silent. But she hadn't given up. "Paul, you know what I think?" she said. "Maybe you don't even realize it. Maybe it's buried somewhere deep in your subconscious. But I still think some part of you is attracted to this man's lifestyle."

Paul sat down as well. "Come on, Evelyn, we had that conversation months ago."

"So why are we having it again?"

Things had gone even worse than he'd thought they would. He knew he was not going to change her mind no matter how long they traded barbs. He had given his word. *And* he believed he was right. '*Time to get off the pot*,' he thought.

"Evelyn, despite me saying how hard this was for me, you make it sound as though it was an easy decision. Well, it wasn't but I made it – and I'm not changing my mind. I already told her I would help."

"Then what's the point of this discussion?"

"I'd like you to try to understand. I mean, you're sitting there now because of him."

"And there are two other people who aren't sitting here because of him."

"Evelyn, please…"

She stood once more. "I'm sorry, Paul. I've tried but I just can't."

"So, where does that leave us?" he said, standing to face her.

"It leaves you with him. And me – well, it leaves me somewhere else."

"Evelyn…"

"I better leave. I think I can hear your friend calling."

"Evelyn, wait."

But it was too late. She had already turned and walked away.

Chapter Six

After slapping some sense into his nephew, it was time for Gus to pay a visit to Rico. Larry had told him that he and Koblentz were just having a spirited conversation when Rico butted in for no reason. The version that witnesses gave to the newspapers and the police was that Larry had been the aggressor and Gus knew his nephew all too well. He believed what he read in the papers. And he knew Rico. Rico wasn't about to start a ruckus with a snot-nosed kid like Larry for no reason. So, despite what he'd said, Larry had indeed been the aggressor. That made a difference. It would make it harder for Rico to walk away. True, three guys were dead and, although badly wounded, Rico was still alive. But there was the principle of the thing. And Rico was big on principles.

The day after his talk with Larry, Gus entered the lobby of the hospital and got Rico's room number from the receptionist. Then he went to a courtesy phone and dialed.

"Yeah," Rico answered.

"This is Gus."

"And?"

"Well, I'm downstairs. Can I come up?"

"You alone?"

"Yeah. Just me."

"Come on up."

A few minutes later Gus appeared outside Rico's room and knocked on the open door. "It's me, Rico. Okay if I come in?"

"Knock yourself out."

Gus entered, approached Rico's bed, and stood beside it. "How you feelin'?"

"Good. How *you* feelin'?"

"Great."

"You look nervous."

"Me? No, I'm not nervous."

"Pull up a chair."

Gus dragged a chair over from a corner of the room and sat. Rico eyed him for a moment and re-lived the day of the shooting from the point when he saw the three men advancing toward him until the point when his memory failed him. *'This is personal. No deference and no respect. And Gus better not expect either.'*

"What took you so long to get here?"

"Well, I didn't figure you could have any visitors right away."

"Well, *I* figure a couple o' days should give you enough time to get your story straight."

"Now hold on. What story?"

"I don't know, Gus. It's your story."

"There's no story, Rico."

"Then let me have it straight. Who's that pipsqueak whose clock I shoulda cleaned the minute I laid eyes on him?" Gus hesitated. "Come on, spit it out. You came here to talk about somebody, Gus, and I don't think it was the three stiffs in the morgue."

Gus didn't know why but he was having second thoughts about coming clean with Rico, which didn't make sense. There wasn't a snowball's chance in hell that Rico wouldn't find out sooner or later. "Name's Larry Cosgrove," he blurted out. "He's my nephew. My sister's kid."

"That figures. How come I never heard of him?"

"He's from outta town. Only been here a couple o' months."

"What the hell were they doin', packin' all that heat anyway? A sawed-off shotgun, seriously? Why?"

"They were gonna knock over some joint in Hammond later that afternoon just before closing. They stopped to get some liquor for the celebration later."

"Idiots," Rico said. He locked his fingers behind his head and leaned back against the pillows propping him up. "So, what does he want, Gus?"

"He wants to live."

"I'm shocked. What else?"

"He wants to call it even."

"That's easy for him to say. He didn't get all shot to hell."

"Rico, for Christ sakes, he's just a kid. A little hot-headed maybe, but still just a kid."

"Bullshit. The only kid there was the boy Larry knocked on his ass."

"Rico, give me a break here."

Rico paused for a moment, thinking. "Larry made a few friends in a couple o' months. Three of 'em get wasted, you figure somebody's nose has gotta be outta joint."

"Sam was the only one who had any family."

"You mean Cleveland."

"Yeah, he just got out."

"From where?"

"Soledad."

"Not my favorite place."

"Mine either."

"He wanna call it even, too?" Rico asked.

"I got it covered," Gus said.

Rico's brow furrowed darkly. "You talk to him?"

Gus started to lie but thought better of it. "Not yet, but I'm sure we can work it out."

"You square this with him and *then* we'll talk about Larry."

Gus stood. "If that's all it's gonna take..."

"I didn't say it was over. I said we'd talk. And by the way, that wasn't much of a story. Maybe it didn't take a couple o' days to dream it up. Maybe you just thought if you waited long enough, I might croak in here."

Gus managed a faint smile. "Thought never crossed my mind, Rico."

He stood and headed for the door. He turned to face Rico as he reached it. "Incidentally, one of the boys has a cousin lookin' for a divorce lawyer. That lawyer you know, Elliott – he do that kind of work?

Rico shot him a hard stare. "No."

"Okay, just askin'."

"And Gus, the next time you drop by, call ahead like you did this time. It makes me feel better."

Gus smiled weakly and hurried out the door. When he was gone, Rico removed his Sig from beneath the bed covers and re-attached it to the underside of the bed.

Cleveland Russell, a brawny forty-year-old African American who stood a little over six feet and weighed in at around two hundred and twenty pounds, had been out on parole for only a little over a month when word reached him that his younger brother Sam had been killed. He had kept his nose clean inside and had been rewarded with a parole after only six years. He and Sam had been close, and both had entered the embrace of crime as a way of life in their mid-teens, the way a lot of their friends had, starting with petty stuff and working their way up from there. It was a short distance from purse snatching and shoplifting to burglary and armed robbery. When they weren't working for Gus, they mostly stole cars, and delivered them to chop shops where each of them worked from time to time.

Leaving their childhood home inherited from their deceased parents in Sam's care, Cleveland had moved to Los Angeles three years before he went to prison. He had been lured there by a friend who raved about the sunny weather and the good-looking women. Still, he only intended to stay for a few years. It would be a nice change of pace from the cold and wind, or as Lou Rawls called it, "the Hawk, the almighty Hawk," that characterized Chicago's brutal winters.

He got a job at a gas station working as a mechanic, and he and his friend boosted cars and burglarized houses on the side. The owner of the gas station was going to retire soon and talked to Cleveland about taking over the business. At first, he didn't give the idea any serious consideration, but then it dawned on him that maybe he could make a go of it and perhaps even leave the criminal life behind him. He might even convince Sam to come out and join him. It was right about that time that he sat in on a friendly crap game. One of the players didn't like losing and tried to walk away with Cleveland's winnings. Being no pushover, that didn't sit well with Cleveland, and the next thing he knew, he was behind bars doing fifteen years for manslaughter.

His parole officer drove him to the Greyhound bus terminal to catch a bus to Chicago. With his help, Cleveland had made initial contact with a funeral home.

"You've got three weeks to take care of your brother's funeral arrangements and to put his things in order. I don't know if that's enough time, but it's the best I could do."

"Okay," was all Cleveland said, in a flat voice devoid of emotion.

"I'm just your parole officer, so what the hell do I know. But I'm gonna say it anyway. Nothing you can do is gonna bring your brother back, but you can sure bring yourself right back to prison. If you so much as dream about getting even with the guy who killed him, we'll have you back in Soledad before you wake up. Understood?"

"Yeah," Cleveland said and turned away.

"Good. Then I'll see you in three weeks." The parole officer paused then, to wait until he regained Cleveland's full attention. When Cleveland turned to face him again, he added, "And, Cleveland, good luck to you. Something tells me you're gonna need it."

Chapter Seven

Paul had not seen or spoken to Valerie Wallace since their awkward meeting at their high school reunion a few days earlier. Despite the passage of time since high school and all of the milestones in his life that followed, he had to admit that she still held a peculiar fascination for him. After all, she had been his first love, albeit unrequited, and he'd been smitten for years, as evidenced by the fact that he still remembered her childhood phone number, a number he'd never dialed a single time. But the whole thing was silly, a teenage crush, and he was glad that Evelyn had forced him to get it off his chest so that he could put it behind him once and for all.

And then he and Evelyn had that ugly fight over his "guardian angel", so to speak, whom he now knew as Richard Sanders, aka Rico. Later that same night, for no reason he could fathom, as he lay in bed, Valerie had briefly come to mind again, her image fleeting, like a distant comet racing across the starlit sky. Afterwards he had banished her from his thoughts once more and rolled over to sleep. Then something unexpected happened.

The following night, she called.

Dressed in a shockingly scant negligee and lying face down on her bed, she'd dialed Paul's number and purred into the phone. "Do you know who this is?"

The caller ID read "private" so, as was his custom, Paul hadn't intended to answer. But some impulse had led him to pick up. "Excuse me?" he said.

"Now you've hurt my feelings."

"Valerie?"

"That's better. You had me worried. How are you?"

"I'm fine. This is a surprise."

"It shouldn't be. It was good to see you after all those years."

"I see."

"Do I detect a note of skepticism?"

Paul perked up. He transferred the book he was reading from his lap to a side table next to his easy chair. "Of course not. So, how are you?"

Valerie rolled over and toyed with the phone line, playfully rolling it around a finger and unrolling it again and again. "I'm bored out of my mind. Joe is out of town with his bowling league – again, and all my girlfriends are busy with one thing or another. So, I'm cooped up in this big old house... all by myself." She waited for Paul's reaction and, not getting one immediately, she added, "And I thought... that if you weren't busy..." She left the thought dangling in midair.

"Yes...?"

"... that we could get together and talk about old times – or something."

"I don't know, Valerie..."

"I'm not interrupting anything, am I?"

"No, I was just catching up on some work," he lied.

"I thought you'd be happy to hear from me."

"I am, but..."

Valerie sat up in bed and folded her legs in front of her. "You don't have a date with that cute girlfriend, do you?"

"Actually, I should explain something to you about her and me."

"Tell me later. I'm not going to get you in trouble with her, am I?"

Paul stood and unconsciously meandered over to the window and looked out at nothing in particular. "Of course not, but –"

"It's settled then... unless you'd rather not..."

"No. I'd like to."

"Really?" she said.

"Really."

"Good. Would you like to stop by here?"

He returned to his chair, sat, and loosened his collar. "I don't think that would be a good idea."

"Why, Paul, whatever are you thinking? This is just a get-together between two old friends."

"Valerie, I..."

"But if it'll make you feel any better, I'll stop by your place. Is that better?"

"That's fine. It'll be good to see you."

Valerie lay on her back, knees up, twirling her ankles and smiling to herself. "Don't worry, Paul. I just thought it would be nice to talk about old times. Maybe we could go out for a drink or something."

"Sure. When should I expect you?"

"Is an hour okay?"

"See you then."

Forty-two hours and thirty-five minutes after Cleveland left LA, his bus pulled into the station in Chicago. It was early evening. He checked his pants pocket for the first time since he'd left LA and made sure he still had the extra key to the house which he and Sam shared after his parents died. He still had a couple of friends he could have called and asked to pick him up from the bus station, but he decided to splurge and take a cab.

The house was a three-bedroom frame structure with a wide front porch extending a third of the width of the house. From the outside, it didn't seem to have changed much since Cleveland left, except it appeared to have been painted a few years earlier. It looked like Sam had taken pretty good care of the place.

When the cab arrived, a next-door neighbor, a tall, thin African American man in his sixties, peered through his curtains and, recognizing Cleveland, came out to say hello before Cleveland could make it to the stairs that led to the porch.

"Cleveland, is that you?"

"Yeah, it's me, Mr. Grimble."

"I'm sorry about your brother."

"Thanks."

Grimble could tell that Cleveland was not in the mood for idle chit-chat. "Well, it looks like you're just getting in, so I won't keep you."

Cleveland turned to walk up the stairs when he noticed for the first time that the lawn had been neatly mowed and trimmed. "Who cut the grass?"

"Oh, that was me," Grimble said.

"Thanks," Cleveland said. "How much do I owe you?"

"Not a thing."

"You sure?"

"You didn't ask me. I volunteered. If you want me to keep doing it, though, we can talk about it later."

"'Preciate it," Cleveland said and continued up the stairs and into the house. As was true with the exterior of the house, the interior was reasonably well maintained. Nevertheless, a musty, unlived-in smell hung in the air. *'Sam must not have spent too much time here. Probably runnin' the streets.'* he mused, releasing a quiet sigh.

Cleveland opened the windows and then headed upstairs to shower off the accumulated aromas that clung to his body after spending two days and four hours on a crowded bus, whose air conditioning only sporadically worked. Then, changed and refreshed, he made the several blocks' trek to the neighborhood bar.

Inside, Cleveland took a seat at the bar and ordered a beer. It was early and the place was mostly empty. As the bartender filled his glass, Cleveland casually remarked, "I heard there was some bullets flyin' around here a few days ago."

"You heard right."

"So, what happened?"

"Who wants to know?"

"Is it some kinda secret?"

"No, but..." The bartender stared at him, searching for recognition. "Cleveland."

"Russell? Cleveland Russell?"

The bartender offered his hand and the two men shook.

"I'm really sorry about your brother," the bartender said. "But you need to talk to somebody else about this."

"What do you mean?"

"You know Gus Chakiras, don't you?"

"I heard the name."

"Hold on a minute." The bartender went to the other end of the bar and punched Gus's number into his cell. When Gus answered, he said, "He's here."

Thirty seconds later, the bartender returned to Cleveland. "He's sending a car. It'll be here in a minute."

Cleveland said nothing, took a sip of his beer and stared straight ahead.

Chapter Eight

Evelyn and Paul had been together for almost three years, not counting the years they knew each other in college before they were a couple. In college Paul had fallen hard for her but, rebelling against the strict upbringing she'd received from the doting parents of an only child, she had rejected him in favor of Robert, who was precisely the kind of guy her parents had shielded her from when she was in high school. He was fun-loving, gregarious, and a smooth talker, but ultimately, he lacked both character and scruples. Once they were married, not only did it become clear he was a thief, but he became even more of a womanizer, a heavy drinker, and an insatiable gambler, all traits Evelyn either had failed to see or had blindly ignored. After a few years filled with futile attempts to change him, Evelyn realized her mistake, but by this time, Paul was happily married. But deep inside, even as his marriage thrived, he had never stopped carrying a torch for Evelyn, though their paths diverged, and he lost contact with her.

Once Rico killed mob boss Frank Litvak, to prevent him from killing Paul and Evelyn, they never expected to see or hear from him again. However, a year later, owing to a tangled set of circumstances, he had re-appeared.

The teenage daughter of one of Paul's neighbors had witnessed a carjacking during which the driver was accidentally killed by the carjacker, a seventeen-year-old boy. Unbeknownst to the boy, he had a secret protector, one Howard Forester, another mob boss, who had his own motives. In a bid to keep the boy out of prison, Forester hired a hit man named D'Angelo to kill the girl, the only witness to the carjacking.

As the girl's parents were in the middle of a divorce and her mother was out of the country, Paul and Evelyn became her temporary guardians after D'Angelo accidentally killed her father while attempting to kill her. Already there had been bad blood between D'Angelo and Rico, but when Paul foiled D'Angelo's second attempt on the girl's life, he determined to kill both Rico and Paul, whom he perceived to be a friend of Rico's. After Rico found out about D'Angelo's plans, he warned Paul. Paul then had an encounter with D'Angelo when he broke into Paul's apartment, and at first Paul thought he had killed him. In fact, Paul had only wounded D'Angelo and, while Rico tried to keep his involvement a secret from Paul, he had been waiting outside Paul's building and, unbeknownst to Paul, had finished D'Angelo off.

In short, Rico had saved Paul's life twice and wanted nothing in return. But all Evelyn knew was that Rico was bad news, and she certainly didn't want Paul to get involved with him again, no matter the circumstances.

Since their chance meeting in Honolulu, Paul and Evelyn had been through hell, what with murderers and mobsters lurking around almost every corner it seemed, and yet somehow, they had muddled through and managed to fall deeply in love. Evelyn did not intend to let a third encounter with Rico finally drive Paul and her apart for good. But one of them had to be big enough to start the dialogue. She decided she would be the one, even if it meant an apology from her without a reciprocal one from him. It was a big concession: she was as proud as he was. But if it meant saving their relationship, she was willing to try. She just hoped Paul would be willing to meet her half-way. As she drove to their townhouse, she rehearsed what she intended to say to break the ice.

Evelyn's car was three houses away when she saw a female figure that seemed vaguely familiar walking toward the door of their townhouse. Curious, she stopped the car and turned off her headlights. The porch light came on, illuminating the face of the person she thought she'd recognized. It was Valerie, as unmistakable then as she had been the night Evelyn first laid eyes on her at Paul's high school reunion.

Paul opened the door, smiled, and let her in. The door closed behind them. A look of shock and disappointment washed over Evelyn's face. She sat staring at the door for a long moment. Finally, she turned the headlights back on and slowly started to drive away. Tears flooded her eyes and slowly worked their way down her cheeks. A jolt of rage and betrayal surged through her and she floored the gas pedal, burning rubber.

Chapter Nine

The man who walked into the bar said simply that Gus had sent him. He knew who Cleveland was because the bartender nodded in his direction when the man appeared in the doorway. Cleveland finished off his beer and, without a word, followed the man to his car. After the man drove off, he turned to Cleveland and asked, "Long trip?"

"Long enough," Cleveland said, and that was the extent of the conversation between the two men until they reached Gus's modest home fifteen minutes later.

"This is it," the man said.

"Thanks," Cleveland said and headed for the door as the man drove off.

Cleveland rang the doorbell and Larry rose from his chair and opened the door. The living room of Gus's single-family, one-story home was neat, clean and simply furnished. He and his wife lived there alone. They could have easily afforded a much nicer home in a much nicer neighborhood, but that would have been ostentatious, and Gus was not an ostentatious man. He was from the old school of mobsters who believed in maintaining a low-key lifestyle so as not to attract undue attention. He was not alone in believing that John Gotti's downfall was attributable in large part to the publicity generated by his flamboyant lifestyle.

"Come on in," Gus said and rose from his easy chair. He met Cleveland half-way and they shook hands. "This is Larry Cosgrove, my nephew."

Wary of each other, Larry and Cleveland didn't shake but acknowledged each other with a nod. With the wave of his hand, Gus motioned to them to have a seat on a couch. They sat and he returned to his easy chair facing them.

"What do your friends call you, Cleveland?" Gus asked.

"Just Cleveland."

"Okay, Cleveland. How about a drink?"

"A beer would work."

"Larry, get him one outta the fridge, would ya?"

Larry got up and went to the kitchen for the beer.

"How was your trip, kid?" Gus asked.

"Okay, I guess."

"How many years you do?"

"Six."

"That's a long time. I never did more than four at a stretch. And that guy you took out – from what I heard, he was askin' for it."

Cleveland didn't answer but just then, Larry returned with two opened bottles of beer, handed one to Cleveland, and returned to his seat.

Cleveland took a swig from his bottle, leaned forward, and said to Gus, "So tell me. What happened?"

Gus recounted Larry's version of the shootings, according to which Rico had instigated the whole thing. When he finished, he turned to Larry. "Is that about right, Larry?"

"Yeah, but Rico's next stop shoulda been the morgue."

Gus cast an irritated look in Larry's direction. *'You knucklehead. We just talked about this.'* he thought. Cleveland sat back in his chair, took another swig from his bottle. Then he said matter-of-factly, "My parole officer got the Chicago paper for me. It said you started it."

The comment came out of left field. They hadn't counted on Cleveland reading news reports of the killings, but they should have. Larry scrambled for a comeback. He had none except the old cliché: when in doubt, deny. "That's bullshit," he shouted. But he didn't know where to go from there. He looked nervously to Gus, who tried to stall for time.

"Wait a minute, Cleveland," Gus said angrily. "This is my nephew. If he says that's the way it went down, then that's the way it went down." Cleveland stared at them implacably. Gus paused, hoping Larry could come up with something fast.

It was enough time for a practiced liar like Larry to invent a reasonable explanation. "The paper didn't get my side of the story," he said. "Rico knew those witnesses, and the ones he didn't, he paid off."

Now it was Cleveland's turn to pause. Gus and Larry exchanged glances, expecting pushback. But none came. "I don't give a shit," Cleveland said. He shrugged his huge shoulders. "He killed my brother and I don't much care how it happened."

"I figured that's the way you would feel," Gus said, relieved that Cleveland was not blaming Larry but apprehensive about his chances of convincing Cleveland not to retaliate against Rico. "But the point is, though, I don't want a war over this. It was a lousy misunderstanding, whoever started it. Larry and the old guy had some words, is all. Then Rico pokes his nose in, and your brother and the other two guys try to help Larry and, Christ, nobody shoulda got killed behind it, that's all."

"Mr. Chakiras –"

"Gus. Call me Gus."

"– Gus, you said it was a misunderstanding. I can appreciate that. But misunderstanding or not, my brother is still dead." Cleveland's voice was flat.

"Okay, kid, let me put it to you this way. The first thing is, I know Larry here since he was a baby, and I knew your father, too. I don't want anything to happen to either one of you. But like I told Larry, you go up against this guy, you don't walk away. Neither one of you. That right, Larry?"

"Sure, Gus," Larry said halfheartedly. That pitch hadn't worked on Larry the first time, and it wasn't working now. Deep resentment colored his face. Gus didn't see it because he was concentrating on selling Larry, but Cleveland did.

"He goes to take a piss, he holds his dick with one hand, just like I do," Cleveland said.

Gus sighed heavily. He knew he was making sense and that what he was saying was crystal clear, but neither of these two numbskulls was listening. "I can tell you got a one-track mind, just like Larry. You both think you're indestructible. So, let me tell you the second thing. This neighborhood is like my house. Take a look around." He leaned forward and made a sweeping gesture with his arm. "Nothin' special, but it's nice and clean. I keep it that way 'cause I gotta live in it. So, I don't want people comin' into my living room and takin' a crap on the floor. 'Cause if they do, I gotta clean it up. Same thing with this neighborhood. You and Larry try to even the score with Rico and somebody's gonna make a mess that I gotta clean up. And I'll be damned if I'm gonna be shovelin' somebody else's shit, that's all."

"I hear you," Cleveland said, "But it just don't sit right, with Sam in the ground and this guy still breathin'."

Gus thought he was making progress. Cleveland was still listening. He settled back in his chair and heaved another deep sigh. "I give it to you straight. Now I want you to just think about it, that's all. And when you make up your mind, come back and see me. We'll talk about it. Is that fair?"

Cleveland stood. He had said his piece. It didn't make sense to press it any further at this point. "We'll see," he said.

Gus also stood. "I take it that's a yes."

"We'll see," Cleveland repeated.

Like Cleveland, Gus felt he had made his point and that was as far as he intended to push things that night. "Okay," he said. "Where you stayin'?"

"At the house."

"Larry will give you a ride. How long you gonna be in town?"

"Don't know yet."

"If there's anything I can do for you while you're here, just let me know. I want you to know I'm sorry for your loss." He reached into his pocket and peeled off five one hundred-dollar bills and stuffed them in Cleveland's shirt pocket before he could object. "Here, take this to tide you over."

"I'm okay."

"Take it," Gus insisted, and put his arm around Cleveland's shoulder and walked him to the door. "I know how it is, just gettin' outta the joint and all. And Cleveland, just think about what I said, okay?"

"Yeah, okay," Cleveland said and walked out the door ahead of Larry.

Larry's car was parked out front, two houses down from Gus's. He and Cleveland walked to the car in silence, but Larry was seething. It had been all he could do to sit still while Gus lectured him for the second time, like some stupid kid. Cleveland could tell that it wouldn't be long before Larry couldn't hold it in any longer. He was a hot-head all right and he didn't believe Larry's story for a second, but it really didn't matter. He couldn't see past the fact that his brother was dead, and his killer had to pay. It was as simple as that.

After Larry started the car and put it in gear, he pounded both hands against the steering wheel and the dam burst. "This neighborhood is like my house," he said, mocking Gus' voice. "He's already shovelin' shit. Rico is callin' the shots, not him."

"What's up with that?" Cleveland asked. "When I was comin' up, Gus ran things around here."

"I guess he just got old – and scared. I heard a while ago Rico took out one of the bosses – a guy named Wilson – 'cause he wanted to do some guy who saved Rico's life – a lawyer, I think. And nobody did a fuckin' thing about it. Then Rico popped John D'Angelo – a pretty tough guy – after D'Angelo whacked Howard Forester and tried to pin it on Rico. Since then everybody thinks he walks on water."

"But you don't," Cleveland said.

"Hell, no." Larry snarled.

"That makes two of us."

Chapter Ten

Paul lay awake in bed staring at the ceiling in the early morning light. Valerie, her clothes neatly folded on a chair, lay next to him, fast asleep. He had succumbed to her unsubtle advances the night before, partly to get back at Evelyn and in part, if he was honest, he had simply surrendered to desire. And to ego. The most seductive girl in his high school class, still capable of attracting hordes of men with barely a wink, had chosen him over all of them, at least for a night.

He had always been the boy scout: physically strong, mentally alert, and morally straight, trustworthy, loyal, helpful, friendly, courteous, kind, obedient, cheerful, thrifty, brave, clean, and reverent. Last night things were turned upside down. He could not resist inhabiting Robert's persona and becoming the kind of bad boy Evelyn had been attracted to all those years ago.

The trouble was that by morning he had become once again who he always was. He couldn't break the mold, any more than Alan Ladd could in the classic western, *Shane*. Now, having tried and failed, he was wracked by guilt. What would he think, he asked himself, if Evelyn had had a one-night stand with an old flame because she was angry with him? It would have broken him.

Valerie stirred, awakened, and turned on her side, facing Paul. "I can hear the wheels turning," she said, seeming to see right through him.

"What do you mean?" Paul asked, knowing perfectly well what she meant.

"The wheels inside your head."

"Just thinking."

"About what?"

"Nothing in particular."

"Then I must be losing my touch," she said playfully.

"It's not that."

"Is that supposed to be a vote of confidence?"

"I didn't mean it like that," he said.

She propped herself up on her elbow. "You aren't sorry this happened? Because that's the vibe I'm getting."

Paul faced her for the first time. "Actually, I am."

A look of disappointment washed over her face. She turned away from him, lay on her back, and folded her arms across her chest.

"Really it was great," Paul said half-heartedly. "You were great."

"But this is the last time, right?"

Now he propped himself up on one elbow and faced her. "Forget about me for a moment. What about Joe?"

"I'm not asking you to marry me, Paul."

"I know that."

"Then Joe has nothing to do with this," she said dismissively.

"Does he know?"

"About me and other men? We don't discuss it over coffee, but yes, he knows."

"And he's fine with that?"

"He's satisfied with his nights out with the boys. I let him have his fun and he lets me have mine." She rolled over and faced him. "Somehow I don't think that explanation solves your problem."

"Well, last night notwithstanding ..."

She smiled. "Lawyer to the end."

He began again. "Despite last night ..."

"Better," she said.

"I'm not in the habit of sleeping with married women."

"So, you were just slumming?" she asked, with a hard edge to her voice.

"I didn't say that," Paul answered, just as seriously.

Valerie smiled and sighed. "Listen up, Paul. I was just teasing. That's what I like about you."

"What?"

"Always so serious."

Paul sat up, back against the headboard, and clasped his hands in front of him. "I need to tell you something – something I should have told you last night when you called."

"Well, tell away."

"Evelyn is not just my girlfriend. We're practically engaged. We had a fight and decided to take some time apart."

Valerie sat up with her back against the headboard next to him. "So, that's why I got lucky," she said playfully.

Paul closed his eyes and shook his head. "I really didn't plan for this to happen."

"You sure know how to keep the compliments coming, don't you?"

He opened his eyes and turned to face her again. "I'm still in love with her, Valerie."

"She might think this is a funny way of showing it."

"Unlike Joe, I suppose."

"You suppose right. But Joe is Joe and Evelyn is Evelyn." She shrugged. "Too bad. We could have had some good times."

She got out of bed, completely nude, walked across the room, and took out two sticks of gum from her purse lying on the chair with her clothes. Then she walked back to the bed and got under the covers with Paul. He tried not to stare, recognizing that she was rather obviously trying to tempt him. He suppressed a smile and looked away as she began her return sashay to the bed. His eyes were elsewhere but, despite his guilty conscience, his mind remained where it had been when he first spied her getting out of bed and crossing the room.

Ever the provocateur, Valerie lifted the covers and glanced underneath. "Just wanted to make sure I still had it."

Paul tried not to, but he blushed. Valerie held out a stick of gum. "Want a piece?" she teased.

"Of gum, you mean," Paul said with a straight face.

"That depends on you."

"A part of me wishes I could."

"You can."

"No, I can't. I tried and I can't accept it as just sex like you do."

She playfully hit him with a pillow. "You did okay last night."

Paul tried and failed to suppress a smile.

"Don't get too cocky, mister."

"Seriously, though. I've been fighting it for as long as I can remember, but I'm just too much of a straight arrow. Always have been, always will be, I guess."

"And that's one of the reasons you're so sexy," she said. "Always were, always will be."

"You're making me blush."

"Then, it's working."

They both laughed. Valerie stopped abruptly. "Now, I'll be serious," she said. "I respect how you feel. I don't completely understand it, but I respect it." She paused and looked into his eyes. "Now, here's one for the road." She kissed him passionately.

He didn't stop her. When she pulled away, he said, "You're tempting me."

"No, I'm not," she said. "Not anymore. But I wish I were."

She rolled out of the bed and disappeared into the shower, leaving Paul alone with his guilty conscience.

Chapter Eleven

The day after his tête à tête with Larry and Cleveland, Gus was feeling confident enough to pay a second visit to Rico. Gus was no fool and the resistance he'd encountered from Larry and Cleveland hadn't gone unnoticed. He knew, of course, that his nephew was an impetuous hothead – a jerk even – but he was family and that was all that mattered. There would be no rough stuff and no need for any really. Maybe he would have to slap him around a little, the way he did before, but he didn't consider that to be "rough stuff." True rough stuff would start with a beating administered by people who knew what they were doing, and if necessary, it might escalate to someone smashing a kneecap with a baseball bat. No, none of that would be necessary with Larry. Nor was anything like that possible, as long as his sister was around.

Cleveland, by contrast, was a bit of an enigma. Gus hadn't seen him in years, and grief could do funny things to a guy. Surely, though, he was someone who ultimately could be reasoned with. If not, there were other methods of dealing with him, up to and including a bullet in the head. Unfortunately for Cleveland, he wasn't the spoiled son of Gus's favorite sister.

Per Rico's instructions on his last visit, he called from downstairs to announce his arrival, and Rico gave him the okay to come up. When Gus entered the room, Rico was sitting up in bed waiting for him. "He got in last night," Gus said, without prefacing the statement with a greeting.

"I'm fine. How about you?" Rico said.

'*You smart-ass motherfucker!*' Gus said to himself. But aloud he simply said, "I meant to ask. I guess I forgot my manners."

"No worries," Rico said. "I was just pulling your chain."

Gus relaxed. He dragged a chair across the floor from a corner of the room, deposited it next to Rico's bed, and sat.

"Have a seat," Rico said, deadpan. Gus got the joke this time and laughed. Rico let him but he never cracked a smile, which irked Gus. After he had squirmed for a few seconds, Rico said, "So, tell me."

"Like I said, Cleveland got in last night."

"And?"

"Me and him and Larry had a nice sit down. He didn't like it, but he'll play ball."

"You sure about that, Gus?"

"You can take it to the bank."

"What about Larry?"

"He'll do what he's told and like it."

"He better."

After their brief conversation Gus excused himself and left. Rico immediately called Jean. Once they had exchanged greetings, he said, "Call off your lawyer friend –"

She interrupted. "Why do you keep saying he's *my* friend?"

"'Cause he's not *my* friend."

"Rico, if I wasn't hearing you, I wouldn't believe it. What difference does it make?"

"None. Now quit yappin' and listen. We don't need to use his place. These guys are done."

"Are you sure?"

"Yeah, I'm sure. They're done. And another thing. Before I got this news, the nurse came by and dropped some more good news in my lap."

"What did she say?"

"She said you can come over and help me get outta this place."

When Cleveland and Larry parted, they agreed that they would hold off on settling their score with Rico until he was released from the hospital. Larry would keep tabs on the hospital and let Cleveland know. In the meantime, Cleveland got Larry to agree that he would try to bring Gus around or, failing that, figure out a way to smooth things over with him. Cleveland was determined to make things right for his brother, but there was no sense in getting on the wrong side of Gus if it could be avoided. Although Larry ostensibly agreed, his agreement was merely patter from a practiced liar. In fact, he was far less concerned about Gus than Cleveland was, because his mother was Gus's favorite sister, and he had successfully leaned on that relationship more than once.

The next day Cleveland took a chance that an old friend would still be working at the same neighborhood drug store she worked at when he left town years earlier. It was about a fifteen-minute walk from his house.

When he reached the drug store, he saw that the owners had expanded it by purchasing the building next door, which formerly housed a laundromat, and that they had erected a spiffy new neon sign that announced the name of the store: Washington Drug. So far, by dint of the expansion, other innovations, and customer loyalty, the owners had managed to fend off the withering competition from regional and national chains that had either acquired or driven out of business so many other small neighborhood drug stores in the city.

He went inside and glanced behind the checkout counter. He was in luck. She was waiting on a customer and, as he'd hoped, didn't notice him as he walked down the nearest aisle toward the back of the store. Now he would be able to surprise her. He picked up a tube of toothpaste and headed toward the front of the store. He stood well behind the one other person in line and took the opportunity to admire her. She was short, petite, and pretty. Her naturally curly hair, which was shorter than Cleveland remembered, accentuated her mocha complexion. Other than the length of her hair, she had changed very little.

When she finished with the customer in front of him, he walked forward and faced her. A look of puzzlement and surprise registered on her face, but it rapidly morphed into one of happiness. Her eyes sparkled and a broad smile emerged.

Seeing her reaction, Cleveland just grinned.

"Cleveland! I can't believe it!"

"I figured you might still be workin' here. How are you?"

"Me? I'm fine. But, how are you? When did you get … back in town?"

Cleveland noticed that she started to ask when he'd gotten out of prison. "That's okay. I got out a while ago. And I got back in town last night."

"Are you okay?"

"Yeah, I'm all right." He paused a moment. "I guess you heard about Sam."

"Yes, I did. I'm so sorry, Cleveland. Is that what brought you back to town?"

A customer got in line behind Cleveland and he stepped to one side to let Sadie wait on her. When she was finished, he returned and stood next to the register. He rested a hand on the counter. "Sam is not the reason I came back, I mean, not because of what happened to him. I came for the funeral and to take care of the house, but that's all."

"Straight up – that's all?" she asked hopefully.

"Straight up."

That brought a smile to her face. "I'm glad. It's really good to see you. Will you be in town long?" Her tone was optimistic.

"It depends, I guess."

"On what?" she asked mischievously.

"Oh, on a lot of things."

She gently rested her left hand on his. "On what?" she teased.

He had stopped listening. He noticed the ring on her finger. "Engaged or married?"

"Married," she said, removing her hand. "Almost twelve years ago. But –"

"Must've been just after I went to LA," he said with a tinge of disappointment.

She walked around the counter and stood next to him, side by side. "Cleveland… He died last year, about this time. Car accident. I wear the ring partly out of respect for him and partly to keep the wolves away."

"Wow. I'm sorry … Kids?"

"Two girls. Melissa and Sarah."

"How old?"

"Seven and four."

"You makin' it okay?"

"Yeah. There was some insurance money after the accident, and Ma helps out a lot… Cleveland, you never said how long you would be in town."

"Well, I'm on parole, so I can't stay long. With Sam gone, I guess I gotta figure out what to do with the house and all."

She turned to face him. "A lot of memories in that old house."

"Tell me about it," he said, musing.

"Remember those parties you and Sam used to throw in the basement?"

He turned to face her. "Yeah, I remember. 'Specially those slow dances with you."

"It was a different time then, wasn't it?" she said softly.

"Yeah, a *real* different time."

She smiled, reminiscing, and they were both silent for a long moment. Finally, she asked, "Cleveland… Did you meet somebody out there? In L.A.?"

He was surprised by the question but answered quickly. "No, not really. I mean, I wasn't a monk or nothin'. But nobody like you."

She blushed and playfully poked him in the chest with a finger. "Then why didn't you stay in touch?"

"Hell, didn't you just tell me you got married right after I left?"

"And didn't you just tell me you didn't know about that? I got married *because* you left."

"Sadie, you know there wasn't any future in it. You did the right thing, gettin' married like you did. You were happy, weren't you?"

"He was a good man and I have my beautiful babies. But if you had tried..."

Cleveland rested his hands on her shoulders and looked into her eyes with sadness. "Not hearin' from me was the best thing that could've happened to you."

"That's always been your problem. You doubted yourself so much that you always stayed in trouble."

"Could be. But that was trouble you didn't need."

"Maybe prison was a good thing, if that's all behind you now." She paused a moment. "Cleveland, it *is* all behind you now, isn't it?"

He removed his hands from her shoulders. "Definitely."

She took his hands in hers. "Good. Then I want you to come over for dinner tonight and meet my two daughters. We'll talk about old times."

"You sure?"

"Sure, I'm sure."

"Okay. It's a date."

Sadie stopped him just as he was about to walk out the door. "Oh, I almost forgot. When is the funeral? I'd like to come."

"In about a week. I'm still working on the details. I'll let you know. And thanks for wanting to come."

At first Cleveland didn't know exactly why he had lied to Sadie. He had been thinking about her since he left Chicago for L.A. In fact, thinking about her in prison had helped to keep him from going insane. Until their talk, he didn't think there was any real chance that they could pick up where they'd left off before he came to L.A. all those years ago. Now she might be offering him that opportunity. Maybe he could rekindle his relationship with her after all. That prospect, though, wasn't enough to cause him to waiver in his determination to settle the score with Rico, because, although he didn't yet know how, he planned to get away with it. Despite his recent stretch in Soledad – so fresh in his mind that the scent of the place still burned his nostrils – he had the mindset of a career criminal who never thinks he's going to get caught and who, once caught the first time, nevertheless returns to the same life of crime and vows that he won't ever be caught again. That's why he'd lied to Sadie. But she would never know.

Chapter Twelve

The day after his tryst with Valerie, Paul made a point of getting to work earlier than usual. He was hoping that, like some talisman, drowning himself in work would ward off the guilt he felt because of his betrayal of Evelyn. And a betrayal was exactly how he characterized what had happened. Yet, despite not trying to rationalize it the way he was sure his classmate Lloyd would have, for instance, as he sat at his desk, he could almost hear Lloyd whispering in his ear:

'After all, Paul, you had the better of the argument about Rico, but despite that fact, it was Evelyn, not you, who stormed out of the house in a huff. Even so, you had had no intention of even looking at another woman, much less sleeping with anyone. That was Valerie's idea, not yours. And how were you supposed to know that's what she had in mind when she called? You aren't a mind reader, after all. Then, what were you supposed to do when she practically invited herself over? Tell her she should go away? And what were you supposed to do when she said she was too sleepy to drive home and asked if she could stay over? Make her get behind the wheel anyway? And when she practically forced herself on you... well, what were you supposed to do then? Why, you resisted, of course. You did resist, didn't you...?'

If he could say all of those things and convince himself that he believed even half of them, maybe he could feel better about himself. But he couldn't honestly say or convince himself to believe any of it. He had betrayed Evelyn and that's all there was to it. He didn't know how he was going to make peace with her, but at least he had made a kind of tentative peace with himself by acknowledging the obvious. It was only the first step. It was enough, though, for him to begin to compartmentalize the incident and get down to work. He could start tormenting himself all over again when he saw Evelyn face to face and had to figure out what, if anything, to say to her about Valerie.

After shunting these unpleasant thoughts to the side, he had just started to get some work done when his phone rang. The caller ID told him it was Bryson Barnes, the managing partner of his firm. After they exchanged greetings, Barnes said cryptically, "People say it all the time but it's really true." Paul furrowed his brow and waited for the punch line. "What I mean is," Barnes continued, "That it's a small world. People say, 'it's a small world' and it actually is. You've never met my grandson Alex, have you?"

"No, I haven't."

"Well, he was in the office yesterday. He and Jim Hart passed you when they were on the way to my office."

"Oh yes, I remember," Paul said. "A boy, around twelve or thirteen. I didn't know he was your grandson."

"Yes, a fine young man. He was shadowing Jim for a school project." He paused a moment as though lost in thought before continuing. "It seems he recognized the young woman you were with. He was very sure. It turns out she made quite an impression on him."

"Oh ..."

"Very striking. A Ms. Webber I believe. At least that's the name she gave to the newspaper reporter. I went back and reread the story after Alex mentioned her. You see, he was playing baseball that day and witnessed her slap one of the men. Another man shooed him away before the shooting started so, fortunately, he didn't see any of it."

Paul was growing impatient. He knew Barnes was leading up to something unpleasant and decided he may as well hurry him along. "Bryson, why don't you just tell me what you're getting at?"

"I won't ask you the reason for Ms. Webber's visit. But in light of the two unfortunate shooting incidents you have already been involved in over the past couple of years, and the resulting negative publicity, which we've talked about before, I want your assurance that nothing of the sort is going to take place again."

That pompous little speech irritated Paul immensely. Barnes knew that most of the publicity had actually been favorable. After the first incident, for example, one headline blared: LAWYER PREVENTS HOMICIDE, KILLS WOULD-BE ASSASSIN. Following the second incident, another headline proclaimed: LAWYER FOILS ATTEMPT ON LIFE OF TEENAGE WITNESS. There were questions in some of the stories about why a partner in a "white shoe" law firm needed to carry a concealed weapon and why he just happened to cross paths on two occasions with figures from Chicago's underworld. But those stories were in the minority. What Barnes didn't like about them was that they implied associations between Paul and, thus, the law firm, and the underbelly of the city. In his judgment, those associations sullied the reputation of a law firm that judged itself by the uniformly high social standing of its corporate clients who, because of their lofty status, occupied a rank far above that of Chicago's lowly plebeians. In a word, Barnes was a snob.

Despite his irritation, Paul decided not to argue the point and tried not to let his annoyance show, succeeding only partially. "Yes, Bryson," he said brusquely. "You have my assurance. Ms. Webber simply wanted some informal advice, which I gave her." He couldn't help adding, "And I'll do my best to keep her from ever darkening the doors of this firm again."

Surprisingly, Barnes didn't react to the jab. He said only, "Thank you."

So, Paul decided to go further and make a comment that he thought Barnes would take the wrong way. "Oh, and by the way," he said, "I'm surprised your grandson lives anywhere near that neighborhood."

Once again Barnes gave no indication that he was insulted by the question or its implication. "Oh, he doesn't," he said blithely. "He was visiting a friend."

"A friend? Really?"

"Yes, our gardener's son."

'*That's commendable,*' Paul thought. '*I wonder if the newspapers know.*'

After his reunion with Sadie, Cleveland took the long way back to his house, slowly reacquainting himself with his old neighborhood. Nothing had changed very much. Nobody earned a lot of money, but most people took pride in their homes which were mostly well maintained. He told himself that that probably explained why his neighbor had voluntarily mowed his lawn.

On the way back he stopped at a corner grocery store and bought a pound of bacon, a dozen eggs, a loaf of bread, a gallon of orange juice, a pound of ground beef, a package of hot dogs, buns, and assorted condiments. He thought that should hold him for a few days, not counting tonight's dinner at Sadie's house.

When he got home, he put the groceries away and plopped down in front of the TV. Before turning it on, he remembered that he had turned his cell off before he left to see Sadie. He turned it on and saw he had three text messages and a voice mail, all from Larry. He ignored the voice mail and returned the call.

"I been tryin' to reach you for a couple of hours," Larry complained, when he answered his phone.

"What's up?" Cleveland said, not bothering to explain why his phone had been off.

"He was discharged this morning."

"Give me thirty minutes. Then swing by. Did you get the piece?"

"Yeah, I got it."

Chapter Thirteen

For Paul, burying himself in work was only effective for a limited amount of time. In the law business, one's workload frequently ebbs and flows, and seldom is there just the right amount. Usually, either there is too much to do or not enough. Lawyers refer to the phenomenon as "feast or famine." Although circumstances could change with one phone call from a client with a huge new assignment, by late afternoon, Paul was approaching a mild period of famine. Without tons of work to occupy him, despite his best efforts, his thoughts returned to Evelyn. He had to see her and try to patch things up.

He didn't want to call in advance. He thought that it would be easier for her to brush him off over the phone than if he showed up in person, so he left work early and took a chance that she would be home. She was staying with a girlfriend in a snazzy apartment building that had been converted into ritzy condos. Visitors had to buzz downstairs in order to gain admittance to individual apartments. He hoped he could talk his way in.

Paul reached the building, a gleaming high rise on the Lakeshore Boulevard just south of the Northwestern University Law School. Inside the foyer he located Evelyn's girlfriend's name and pressed the buzzer. When Evelyn answered, he said, "It's me, Paul. Can I come up?"

"I wish you'd called first," she said.

'*And I'm glad I didn't,*' he thought.

"Now is not a good time, Paul."

'*Very original*,' he thought, not once considering that in fact it might not be a good time. "This won't take long," he said.

'*Very original*,' she thought and wondered how he would react if he discovered that she was entertaining another man. She contemplated repeating, '*Now is **really** not a good time*,' just to make him squirm.

But she didn't and Paul said, "Evelyn, please."

It worked. She buzzed him in. She quickly went to her bedroom, took off her socks and sneakers, jeans, and blouse, and quickly pulled on an oversized sweatshirt like the one Jennifer Beals wore in the movie, *Flashdance*. Then she waited for the knock on the door.

Paul got off the elevator on her floor, walked down the hall, and knocked on her door. She waited almost a minute longer than it would have taken her to meander to the door from the most distant point in the condo. Paul grew suitably concerned and wondered whether he should knock again. Not wanting to appear impatient, he waited.

When Evelyn finally appeared at the door, the loose fitting sweat shirt, which left one shoulder uncovered and stopped only a few inches below her waist, left him speechless, which was fine because, without a word, taking her time, she retreated to the living room, leaving him standing in the doorway. He closed the door, followed her, and watched her sit on one of two love seats, with one leg tucked under her and the other dangling seductively in front of her. He started to sit next to her but warned off by the churlish expression on her face, he thought better of it and instead sat across from her on the other love seat.

"Evelyn, you really look nice," Paul said as soon as he sat down.

"As nice as Valerie?" Evelyn asked, pointedly.

Paul swallowed hard. "Valerie?"

"Yes, that woman at your reunion."

"Of course. Better."

Evelyn seemingly changed the subject, but not really. "How are you making out at the condo all alone?"

Oblivious to the double entendre imbedded in the question, Paul said, "I still think I should have been the one to leave."

"No," Evelyn said icily. "I instigated things, so I'm fine here. Janice is almost never around and as you can see, her apartment is more than large enough for both of us." Situated on the twenty-seventh floor and commanding breathtaking views of the lake from the living room and master bedroom, the two-bedroom condo was suitably luxurious. Decorated with stylish furniture, it was spacious and modern with high ceilings and hardwood floors throughout.

Paul leaned forward. "Listen, Evelyn, I don't think either of us should have to leave. I was hoping we could try to talk things out."

She wanted to cut him off but decided to hear him out. "I'm listening."

Paul stood and slowly paced back and forth. "I don't know if we can ever see eye to eye on this Richard Sanders – or Rico – character. But I do know that I love you and I don't want to lose you."

Evelyn had heard enough. She drew her knees up to her chest, covering them with her sweatshirt, and wrapped her arms around her legs. "You have a strange way of showing it. On second thought, maybe it is the typical way. Why is it that whenever a man and a woman have an argument, the man suddenly has the urge to rush into the arms of another woman?"

Paul stopped pacing. After a pause, he asked, "How did you know?"

"I didn't. Not really. Until now."

"Evelyn, I ... "

"Don't tell me the silver-tongued lawyer is at a loss for words."

"She called – just to talk and – I never expected –"

"*Never expected?* Seriously?" She started to cry. "How *could* you, Paul?"

Paul averted his eyes. He had no answer.

As he waited for Larry to pick him up, Cleveland was preoccupied by two things. First, he had had a bad feeling about Larry from the moment he laid eyes on him, and the sit-down they had with Gus only reinforced his concern. Larry seemed reckless and resentful. Nevertheless, Cleveland was determined to avenge his brother's death, even if it meant working with someone he didn't trust. He would simply have to stay on his toes and watch Larry like a hawk.

Cleveland's other concern was Gus. He was prepared to go through Gus if he had to, but he would prefer to go around him. Larry ought to be able to help, but he was the kind of guy who would throw his own mother to the wolves to get out of a jam, so he couldn't trust Larry to square things with Gus. Cleveland would have to be extremely careful.

Larry pulled up outside Cleveland's house twenty minutes after their phone conversation. After Cleveland got into the car, without exchanging greetings, he asked, "What did you tell Gus?"

"What he wanted to hear."

"And what happens when he finds out?"

"He'll get over it."

Cleveland considered that throwaway response for a moment and decided to let it pass. It wasn't a reassuring answer, but the kid knew his uncle better that Cleveland did. It was yet more reinforcement, though, that he had to be careful in case Larry turned on him.

They had been riding along in silence for only a few minutes when Larry said, almost gleefully, "Well, lookee here. A big insurance policy, just walkin' down the street."

"What are you talkin' about?"

Larry didn't answer. He pulled to the curb abruptly and stopped the car. "Get behind the wheel."

Cleveland wondered what was going on but said nothing and played along. As Larry exited the car, Cleveland slid under the steering wheel. Larry ambled over to the sidewalk and leaned against the car. Fingers clasped in front of his waist, he casually twiddled his thumbs. A moment later, not recognizing Larry, Gabriel Koblentz approached from the opposite direction. Larry stepped in front of him and blocked his path.

"Remember me, pop?" Larry asked, grinning.

Koblentz now recognized him but feigned ignorance. "No," he said firmly.

"That's okay. I remember you." He opened his jacket to reveal a .45 and then opened the back door. "Get in."

Koblentz reluctantly got in the back seat and Larry got in next to him.

"Who is he?" Cleveland asked.

"An old friend. Drive."

Cleveland stepped on the gas and continued toward Rico's apartment. "Is this the old guy?" he asked.

"You guessed it."

Rico lived about fifteen minutes away from Jean in an aging but well-maintained four-story brick structure with one apartment occupying each floor. Anyone entering the building from the street could gain access to each apartment above the ground floor by simply walking up the stairs. The foyer listed the names of the tenants above their mailboxes, but there was no security system requiring visitors to be buzzed in.

Cleveland and Larry mounted the stairs to Rico's third floor apartment with Koblentz in tow. He walked ahead and the other two men followed behind him, Larry prodding him along. When they reached the apartment, they checked for witnesses, removed their guns and stood on either side of the door. They ordered Koblentz to stand in front of the door. Larry looked at Koblentz and nodded. Koblentz knocked three times. There was no answer and Larry nodded again. Koblentz knocked again and again there was no answer.

"You sure he got out today?" Cleveland whispered to Larry.

"Tell him it's you," Larry whispered to Koblentz.

"Hell... Hello... It's Gabe Koblentz."

There was still no answer. Larry and Cleveland exchanged glances and tucked their guns in their belts, each wondering what to do next. Just then a man, about fifty, slight of build, and wearing a checkered flat cap, descended the stairs from the fourth floor. Larry and Cleveland hastily covered their guns with their jackets. When he reached the third-floor landing, the man saw Larry, Cleveland, and Koblentz hovering outside Rico's door. Koblentz struggled to remain calm, but the color had drained from his face and he had begun to shudder slightly. The man became suspicious. The stairwell was several feet from Rico's door, and the man averted his gaze while trying to make his way down the stairs as rapidly as possible. Before he could clear the next flight of stairs, however, Larry yelled. "Hey you!" The man froze. Larry tilted his head toward Rico's door. "You know the guy that lives in here?"

"No, I don't," the man said unsteadily.

Larry pulled back one side of his jacket, revealing his .45 tucked in his pants. "You sure?"

The man hesitated an instant. "Yeah, I'm sure."

Larry removed the .45 and started toward the man, stopping a foot in front of him so that they were practically nose to nose. He then placed the barrel of the gun to the man's temple. "I don't think you heard me."

"He ain't here," the man blurted out.

"Where is he?"

"I don't know! I seen him leave a few minutes ago. Him and a woman. He had a suitcase."

"Sonofabitch!" Larry said to no one in particular. Then he turned to the man. "You sure you don't know where he went?"

"I swear."

"Beat it," Larry said.

The man backed into the stairwell and scampered down the stairs to the street.

Larry rejoined Cleveland and Koblentz. "You know anything about this, old timer?"

"No." His voice trembled with fear.

"I don't believe you," Larry said. "You want me to beat it outta you?"

Cleveland had been standing silently, observing Larry's clumsy, bullying attempts to find out where Rico was. Now he spoke up. "Take a hike," he told Koblentz, jerking a thumb towards the stairs.

Koblentz hesitated a second, his watery eyes wide, and then glanced at Larry for approval. Larry said nothing. Instead, he stared disbelievingly at Cleveland. Seeing the silent interaction between the two men,

Koblentz took advantage of the stalemate and hurried to the stairwell, then down the stairs.

"You wanna tell me what that was about?" Larry asked.

"I'm not going back to the joint for beatin' the shit outta some old man. For Sam, yeah, if I have to, but not for that."

"You worry too much."

"You call it worryin'. I call it thinkin'. I had a lot o' time to think."

Frustrated, Larry shook his head. "So, what do we do now?"

"We wait. He'll be back."

"And what if you ain't here by then?"

"We'll cross that bridge when we get to it."

Paul's cabin was about two hours south of the city. Jean had been driving for about an hour and forty-five minutes when Rico asked how much farther it was.

"Stop being so impatient," Jean said. "You're acting like you have a hot date or something."

"No, I'm acting like I gotta take a leak. I haven't seen a gas station in miles."

"It's only a few more minutes away. Isn't it beautiful out here?"

"It'll do."

"Don't be so grumpy. We're gonna have a great time."

"If we ever get there."

"Rico, you're...incorrigible."

"Incorrigible? I like that."

"Was it a perspicacious observation?"

"Yeah, it was but if you keep usin' words like that, I don't know what I'm gonna do with you."

"Yes, teacher." She grinned and admired the passing scenery again. "I'm glad you changed your mind."

"Like I said before, I always wanted to see the country."

Cleveland had his doubts that Rico would be back before he had to return to Los Angeles, so as he and Larry descended the stairs from Rico's apartment, he stopped Larry and said, "Look, I want this guy as much as you do, probably more. You already said you can square this with Gus. Why don't you talk to him? He probably knows where we can find Rico. Or he knows somebody else who can."

"Fine," Larry said sullenly. But he wasn't about to talk to Gus. He had something else in mind. "Can you make it back to your place okay? I gotta make a run."

Cleveland's house wasn't that far away, and he wondered why Larry couldn't drop him off first. '*Probably still pissed,*' he said to himself. '*But that's his problem, not mine. He wants to do somethin' stupid, let him do it on his own. I gotta look out for me, not him.*'

"Okay?" Larry repeated when Cleveland didn't answer.

"Yeah. Do what you gotta do."

That night Cleveland walked to Sadie's house, a small three-bedroom brick ranch, which was only five blocks away from his. When she opened the door, he could tell that she had gone out of her way to make herself look nice for him. Her mother had watched her daughters while she went to the beauty salon. Petite and pretty, she was wearing a red print dress.

"You look great," Cleveland said.

"Thanks. I'm glad you noticed. I hadn't been to the beauty salon in ages, so I thought this would be a good time to get my hair and nails done."

Once he was inside, Sadie introduced him to her daughters, who had been excitedly awaiting his arrival. When they heard their names, all smiles, each of them ran to their mother and playfully hid behind her. "Cute kids," Cleveland said.

"Girls, what do you say?"

"Thank you!" they said in unison and scurried off to play.

"Long time since I had a meal like that," Cleveland said later, seated on the living room sofa next to Sadie while having a cup of coffee.

"So, you liked it?" Sadie asked.

"Liked it? Does a bear shit in the woods?"

"Cleveland! The girls."

"Sorry. I don't think they heard me." Indeed, the two girls, sitting on the floor several feet away amusing themselves with a word game, seemed oblivious to the conversation between the adults. "Guess I been livin' in the jungle too long. Away from decent folk."

"I think they like you." Sadie said.

"I'm not too good around kids."

"You did fine. Just give it some time." She paused a moment, recognizing the import of her comment. "I almost forgot you have to go back. How much longer will you be on parole?"

"A couple of years."

"That's not so bad."

"Bad enough, but it could be worse."

"Cleveland, you made a joke about a bear in the woods. Well, this thing that got you in prison – it's like an elephant sitting right here on the sofa between us."

"Yeah, I guess it is," Cleveland said, looking down.

When he didn't elaborate, Sadie said, "Well, don't you want to talk about it?"

Cleveland set his coffee cup on the table in front of him and stood and stretched. After a deep sigh, he said, "A man stole some money from me in a crap game. We was both carryin'. I got to mine first."

"Why wasn't that self-defense?"

"He had witnesses. I didn't."

"I'm sorry, Cleveland but you were right about living in the jungle."

"Never thought about livin' no place else."

"You ever think about coming back here – I mean when you get off parole?"

"No, I didn't."

That was not the answer Sadie wanted to hear. She sighed imperceptibly and looked away.

Seeing her reaction, Cleveland added, "I mean, not until tonight."

Sadie turned to face him. "Really?" she said hopefully.

"Yeah, really."

She stood to join him and took his hands in hers. "I'm glad. And I'm proud of you, Cleveland."

"For what?"

"For putting this thing with your brother behind you. I know that wasn't easy. But it's for the best. You don't want to end up back in prison – or worse."

"I've had a belly full of prison. I don't intend to go back. Ever."

Chapter Fourteen

Three days had passed since Rico and Jean arrived at the front door of Paul's secluded cabin. True to form, Rico had continued to improve at a rapid clip. His rib cage was sore, but regular breathing was no longer painful. While a hearty belly laugh would have hurt, that was something Rico didn't have to worry about. His left shoulder was also sore but was mostly pain free, if he moved his arm slowly and avoided reaching above his shoulder. Finally, his right leg still hurt when he walked without his cane, which he was able to do, albeit with a limp, if he moved slowly and deliberately.

Jean had been a big help in changing his bandages, keeping his wounds clean, and pestering him to take his antibiotics and keep off his feet as much as possible. The only time they were apart was when Jean drove to a grocery store a few miles away. She seldom cooked at her apartment, but here she cooked all their meals except breakfast, when they usually had cereal or toast and coffee or orange juice. Jean was not the world's best cook, but her meals handily surpassed anything Rico could have managed, and he silently marveled at her effort.

The two-bedroom cabin, whose signature interior feature was a huge wood-burning fireplace in the living room, was rustic but was equipped with all the modern conveniences except a television and air conditioning. Outside there was a wooden porch that extended across the entire front of the cabin. Two rocking chairs in which Jean and Rico relaxed every day sat on the porch, facing in the direction of the main road that lay some five hundred yards away. A narrow track connecting them to the main road ended in a round-a-bout directly in front of the cabin. Between the cabin and the main road there was a thicket of deep green forest.

As the sun began to set, Rico and Jean sat on the front porch admiring the view. "Too peaceful for you?" Jean asked.

"Is that what it looks like to you?"

Surprised, Jean said, "Don't tell me I'm wrong."

"Okay, I won't."

"Rico, be serious."

Rico paused for a moment to look around one hundred and eighty degrees. "Sometimes I think I could get used to this."

"Just sometimes?"

"Yeah, just sometimes. My ol' man used to take me camping when I was a kid. Christ, it must be twenty-five years by now."

"You never talk about him. Why not?"

"No reason."

Jean was curious but didn't press. "Did you like camping?"

"It was a blast. Real peaceful. Like this. And quiet – except for the insects."

"That sounds nice."

"It was. This isn't too bad either."

Jean stood, strolled a few steps toward the door, and turned to face Rico. "Rico, maybe we could get a place like this. Maybe I could even quit the business and –"

"Whoa, whoa – slow down. Let's just take it in for a minute."

"Okay, but I'm not going to let you forget it." Then a thought occurred to her. "I'm worried about Gabe, by the way. I still can't get through to him."

"Now that you're outta his hair, he's probably out gettin' drunk somewhere."

"I don't think so. That's not him."

"Give the man a chance to breathe. He could use some space."

"I think I'll drive into the city and check on him."

"That's not necessary," Rico said sharply.

Jean returned to her chair and sat facing Rico. "Rico, what's wrong?"

"Nothing. There's just no reason to check on him. Besides, you don't wanna leave me out here all by myself in this helpless condition, do you? Christ, anything could happen to me."

She smiled. For all his seriousness, he had a wry sense of humor. "Okay, I'll give him another day or two. But after that..."

"After that, I'll be ready to get outta here, and we can go together. I'm startin' to get restless."

"But you just said –"

"That was a daydream."

"Not if you don't want it to be."

"It was a long time ago, Jean."

"I'm not letting you off the hook that easily."

"Give it your best shot."

"Don't worry. I will."

They went inside after a while and Jean set about preparing dinner. Nothing fancy: sautéed salmon, baked potatoes, and a salad topped with organic croutons, crushed walnuts, crumbled feta cheese, dried cranberries, and oil and vinegar dressing. Rico sat at the kitchen table and silently observed Jean's cooking skills, which he had grown to appreciate more with every meal.

It was eerily quiet but unless the wind was howling or they were listening to the radio, it was always eerily quiet. Rico sat back in his chair and closed his eyes. They had been closed for only a minute when he heard a faint rustling sound outside. He slowly opened his eyes and, careful not to make a sound, sat up straight. At first, he thought what he'd heard was a squirrel or a rabbit, but in a way he couldn't quite put his finger on, this sound was different. All he could discern was that it was coming from the front of the cabin, and it was getting closer, not rapidly but steadily.

Oblivious, Jean was checking on the baked potatoes in the oven. After closing the door, she casually turned toward Rico. She opened her mouth to say something, but he stopped her by bringing an index finger to his lips.

He closed his eyes for a moment, rapidly thinking. '*Where is my Sig?*' Suddenly, his eyes opened wide. '*Shit! In the bedroom on the dresser.*' Lulled into a false sense of security by the isolation and serenity of the country, he had gotten careless. Any other time (save for the time he had decided to leave his .45 at home when he went to pick up Jean and Koblentz from the supermarket), his Sig would never have been out of eyesight, even when he was alone in his own apartment.

Silently, he quickly weighed his options. He could hobble in to the bedroom himself, but that would mean crossing the width of the kitchen, which he calculated would take about five to seven steps; then turning in to the hall and taking perhaps fifteen more steps to get to the bedroom; and finally taking another five steps or so before he reached the dresser. And then he would have to retrace his steps to get back to the entrance to the kitchen, before proceeding around five to seven steps past it to reach the front door and confront the approaching sound, which an instant earlier he had recognized as footsteps.

No, Jean would have to get the gun and bring it back to him before the footsteps reached the front door, but sooner if possible, in case whoever was out there decided to start shooting before he reached the door. Soon that person would be close enough to hear his voice, but not yet.

"Get my piece," he said, urgently, his voice barely above a whisper.

She had heard him but for some reason, eyes questioning, she hesitated. '*Jean, this is no time to freeze up on me.*' She stared at him and started to ask something, but Rico anticipated her question and answered it.

"In the bedroom on the dresser," he whispered.

She dashed toward the bedroom. Meanwhile, Rico heard the footsteps growing louder. He sprang from his chair as quickly as he could and, after three sizeable steps that taxed his recovering leg, he reached the wall and flipped the switch, turning off the kitchen light.

Jean made it to the bedroom as the kitchen light died. She had only suspected the reason for Rico's alarm, but now she knew; she could hear the footsteps, too. From the doorway she saw the Sig resting inside Rico's shoulder holster, lying on the dresser.

She made it to the dresser in three giant strides. The barrel of the gun was pointing away from her, its handle exposed inside the holster, which rested on top of the elastic strap. *'Should I grab the holster or take the gun out?'* she wondered, her brain whirling. She made the decision in the blink of an eye. She dropped her left hand on the holster to keep it from moving while she simultaneously grabbed the handle of the .45 and jerked it out of the holster. It slid out like a buttered knife between two hotcakes.

Meanwhile, the footsteps continued to grow steadily louder, getting closer with every passing second.

After Rico flipped the switch in the kitchen, leaving his cane behind, he hopped across the kitchen floor and into the hall to await Jean's return. She exited the bedroom a second later, turned, and saw Rico waiting for her, while his eyes focused on the front door. Hearing her enter the hall, he turned and saw her racing toward him.

Now, the footsteps outside reached the front porch.

Then there was a knock at the door.

"Throw it!" Rico yelled.

She did, underhanded, from fifteen feet away. But she didn't have a chance to cradle the .45 in the palm of her hand and gently loft it like a softball. Instead, grasping the handle between her thumb and outstretched fingers, she launched it forward using the same motion she would if she were rolling a bowling ball, but with less force. Unfortunately, that caused the gun to rotate end over end like a hatchet thrown at a target at a carnival. As the .45 traveled toward Rico, turning end over end, he deftly timed the revolutions, caught it by the handle in his right hand, and in the same motion, whirled and pointed it toward the door.

"Who is it?" he asked calmly.

Chapter Fifteen

Jean crept up toward Rico as he waited for the person outside the door to answer. He signaled to her to stay back and lie on the floor with a wave of his free hand then an index finger pointing down.

Then a voice from outside said, "Paul, is that you? It's me, Hank."

This could be a ruse, but Rico doubted it. He relaxed. Larry wasn't smart enough to find out the name of a neighbor who knew Paul and then force him to knock on the door, and he wasn't smart enough to try to impersonate the neighbor, whose voice sounded authentic to Rico. He made his way to the door and peeked through the peep hole. Outside was a scrawny middle- aged man with dark, wavy hair and bulging eyes. He stood about six feet tall and looked to weigh all of a hundred and fifty pounds. He was alone.

Rico nodded to Jean to indicate that everything was all right, and he tucked his .45 in his belt behind his back and covered it with his shirt. He opened the door and stood face to face with Hank Crenshaw, who said, "Hi. I saw the lights and thought Paul and Evelyn were here. I guess I should have called first, but I was already out walking. Name's Hank Crenshaw. I live about a mile east of here."

"Come on in," Rico said courteously, doing his best impression of a middle-class suburbanite spending a few days at a friend's cabin.

"I don't mean to trouble you," Crenshaw said.

"No trouble at all," Rico said, as Crenshaw stepped inside a little awkwardly. "My name is Richard Sanders," he said, extending his hand,

"and this is my wife Jean. I'm one of Paul's partners." They shook hands.

Unsure of Rico's gambit, Jean raised an eyebrow but came forward, shook Crenshaw's hand and said hello.

"I'm recuperating from an operation on my leg and Paul let us have the cabin for a few days. I'm doing better already. Jean was back in the bedroom when you knocked. I got to the door without my cane, but I almost fell in the kitchen. When I reached for the wall to brace myself, I accidentally turned the light off. I got pretty frustrated. You probably heard me yell to her to throw my cane. Sometimes, I guess I can be a little impatient."

"I told you to wait and I would get the door *and* your cane, but you're so stubborn," Jean said, smiling.

"Can I get you a drink, Hank?" Rico asked. Before he could answer, Rico added, "In fact, we're just about to sit down for dinner. There's enough for one more, isn't there, Jean?"

"Well... Yes, I think so," Jean said haltingly.

"Sure, there is," Rico said. "What do you say?"

"Oh, no, I couldn't," Crenshaw said. "That's awful nice of you, but my wife is waiting for me back at our cabin."

"If you'd like to go and get her ..." Rico said.

"That's nice of you but no, but thanks. I just stopped by to say hello. We're actually heading back to the city first thing tomorrow, and we've got a lot to do tonight."

"Maybe some other time then," Rico said. "When do you plan to be back?"

"Oh, not for a few weeks, anyway. It's hard to say."

"Well, we'll probably be gone by then."

Crenshaw checked his watch. "Oh my, I'd better be getting back. It was nice to meet you and tell Paul and Evelyn I said hello."

"Sure thing," Rico said, all civility.

"Good-bye,' Jean said. "Nice to meet you, too."

When Crenshaw was out of earshot, Jean said, "You really laid it on thick."

"I didn't want him to think we'd broken into the place," Rico said. "Besides, it was fun. You think we fooled him?"

"Yeah, but you didn't have to ask him to join us for dinner. What if he'd said yes?"

"No way was that gonna happen," Rico said. "He just stopped by to say hello on a whim. He wasn't gonna invite himself to dinner with a couple of strangers."

"Strangers? By the time you finished talking, he was practically your best friend." She paused to see if that would cause Rico to smile, but his face was a blank page. "Okay, Mr. Know-it-all, if you say so. And by the way, that was a good catch."

"I try."

"Seriously, that thing could've gone off if it had hit the floor, couldn't it?"

"I was pretty sure I'd catch it, but if it had hit the floor, it probably wouldn't have gone off. It doesn't have a manual safety, but it doesn't need one. Four things keep it from going off if you drop it: a de-cocking lever, an automatic firing pin safety block, a safety intercept notch, and a trigger bar disconnector."

"No kidding," Jean said feigning astonishment.

"Well, you asked. I guess all I shoulda said is that as long as you keep your finger out of the trigger guard, the gun won't fire."

"I'll keep that in mind, professor," Jean said. "How about we eat now?"

The following day Jean arose early. She had barely slept the night before. She had to make a decision about something and couldn't make up her mind, so she resolved to try to put it off until morning when, presumably, her mind would be fresh and clear. She was right; sleeping helped. And shortly after sunrise she decided. She showered and dressed as quietly as possible, trying not to disturb Rico. He was such a light sleeper that she was amazed he hadn't awakened. But just as she was leaving the bedroom, she thought she heard him stir. She hurried out to the car and was gone in a flash.

Rico thought he heard something and woke up. He looked next to him and saw that Jean was not there. *'Must be in the bathroom.'* He turned over and went back to sleep.

Evelyn picked up the morning paper outside her door and glanced at the headlines as she walked to her living room and sat on the couch. After Paul's surprise visit five days earlier, they had parted, leaving matters between them unresolved. Paul remained the supplicant, asking when he could see her again. She had put him off, saying she wasn't sure when she would be ready to talk to him again and asking him to wait for her to contact him. Paul had respected that and sent flowers but had otherwise left her alone. She still wasn't sure her emotional wounds had healed sufficiently to allow her to forgive him. Now, as her eyes scanned the articles below the fold on the front page, she saw one that caused her to break the silence between them. She called Paul at work.

"I'm glad you called," Paul said, pleasantly surprised.

"I ... I wish it were just to say hello."

Paul detected a note of alarm in her voice. "Evelyn, what's wrong?"

"Have you seen today's paper?"

"No, why?"

"Isn't 'Gabriel Koblentz' the name of the elderly man who that Rico character was trying to help, when he was shot?"

"Why, yes. What about him?"

"They... They found his body floating in the river. He'd been shot. It's on the front page."

Paul didn't know Koblentz, but the news shocked and saddened him. "Jesus, poor guy... What else does it say?" He remembered that he'd bought the morning paper. "Wait a minute." His eyes searched the room for his briefcase. "I have a copy here. Let me put you on speaker."

Paul put her on speaker and retrieved the paper from his briefcase lying on a chair in front of his desk. He located the article, returned to his seat, and followed with Evelyn as she skimmed it.

"There's not much," Evelyn said. "Just that he was a long-time resident of the city… no relatives located… no suspects… execution-style shooting, a single bullet to the back of the head… Paul, I'm so worried about you."

"Don't be. I'm fine." He was at once pleased that she was concerned enough to call and deeply alarmed that Koblentz's murder might portend further bloodshed between the murderer and Rico, a concern he didn't want to share with Evelyn. But she was one step ahead of him and quickly came to the point.

"But, Paul, he's using your cabin. What if he's next? If they find him there, they won't have any trouble linking you to the cabin. What if –"

"Calm down, Evelyn. I know you're upset but that's a lot of "what ifs." The point of him going out there is they have no way of tracing him there."

"All right, Paul. If you insist on ignoring the fact that you may be in danger, fine. But in the meantime, I'm coming down there." Her voice was tense but resolute.

"It would be great to see you, but you don't have to do that."

"Paul, I'm coming down."

"But, Evelyn, I have appointments …."

"Paul, you know very well you can reschedule them. Now promise me you'll wait for me."

"Evelyn –"

"Please."

"Okay."

"I'm on the way."

As soon as Paul hung up with Evelyn, he called his secretary and asked her to reschedule his appointments for the day. Then he called Rico's cell. Rico picked up the phone, wiped the sleep out of his eyes, and sat up with his back against the headboard. "How did you get this number, counselor?"

"How do you think? Jean gave it to me."

"You and she on a first name basis?"

"That bother you?"

"Should it?"

A part of Paul enjoyed the verbal sparring between him and Rico, who didn't fit the mold of a typical killer, not that Paul knew any. Somewhere inside his psyche there was a conscience, not the same kind of conscience that Paul had, but a conscience, nevertheless. Under different circumstances, it would be interesting to explore it, but now was not the time. "I didn't call to joust with you," Paul said.

"Then, by all means, let's not joust."

Paul got right to the point. "Did you hear about Gabriel Koblentz?"

"Not until now." Rico guessed that somebody had done something to Koblentz, and therefore, as to his condition, there were only two possibilities. "Hurt or dead?" he asked.

"Dead."

"I'll bet he never had a chance." His lips compressed in a tight line.

"He didn't. They found him in the river with a bullet in the back of his head."

"I knew they were layin' in wait for me, but I didn't figure on this, and that cost him. This is gonna be rough on Jean." He hesitated a moment. "You didn't tell her yet, did you?"

"I tried her before I called you. No answer."

Rico scanned the room and seeing no sign of Jean or her phone, he got out of bed. "She's probably communing with nature and doesn't wanna be disturbed." He limped to the bedroom door, stretching out his stiff leg. "I'll go and break it to her now."

"Do you think you're safe there?" Paul asked.

"No reason to find out. We're leavin' as soon as I round her up." Rico made his way to the living room, pulled the curtain back, and looked out the front window. "Hold on a minute. The car is gone."

"Maybe she went to the store or something."

"Not a chance. She's on her way to Koblentz's place."

"How do you know?"

"Because I told her not to." Rico was silent for a moment before continuing. "I hate to say this, counselor, but you gotta come get me."

"Maybe you're wrong. Why don't you try her cell again?"

Rico turned around and his eyes came to rest on a coffee table in the living room. "It wouldn't do any good."

"How do you know?"

"'Cause it's right over there on the coffee table."

"Jesus Christ."

"Ditto."

Under the circumstances, Paul had no choice but to drive to his cabin and pick Rico up. He told Rico he would leave as soon as he could, which would be as soon as Evelyn showed up. When she reached his office twenty minutes later, he took her by the hand and, leading her to the leather couch on the wall in front of his desk, he said, "Let's talk about this." They sat on the couch and he turned to face her. "Do you want to say, 'I told you so?'"

"No, I've learned something," she said. "Some battles you just can't fight. I can't fight that one anymore."

Paul was surprised – and relieved. "I wish none of this had ever happened, but it has. I have to go out there."

"I know."

"About the only way he can get out of there is to hobble to the main road and hitchhike. And if anything happened to Jean because I left him stranded there..."

"You think a lot of her, don't you?"

"I think she's remarkable. Coming here to ask me to help him took guts."

Evelyn stood and went to the window that looked out on the lake. She gazed at it for a long moment before turning to face Paul. "Do you think I've been selfish, Paul?"

"No, I don't. I understand how you felt – feel, I guess. I just didn't think I had any choice." He paused a long moment before continuing. "And, Evelyn, about Valerie, I –"

"Paul, don't. I know we have to talk about it sometime but, please, not now. It's too soon." She measured her next words carefully. "I think we've both grown since Honolulu, but you especially – because you wanted to please me. I don't feel that you're bottling things up and shutting me out anymore. I appreciate that and I don't want a mindless one-night stand to spoil what we have."

"You know, you're pretty remarkable, too." He leaned in and hugged her, and she accepted his embrace. It was a little awkward for both of them, and they separated after a moment.

"No, Paul, I'm not. And I'm not letting you off that easily. We still have to talk about Valerie. But it would have been petty of me to sit around sulking when you might be in danger. And I hope that's not me."

"Don't worry, it's not. Not by a long shot." Paul checked his watch. "Listen, I better get going. The quicker I get him out of there, the better."

"I'm ready when you are."

"Evelyn, there's no reason for both of us to go."

"Paul, you trying to save my life – it seems like ages ago – that's what got you into this mess in the first place. I'm not letting you go alone."

"Evelyn, this could be dangerous."

"I mean it, Paul."

He gave up. He shook his head, frustrated, and went to his desk, opened a drawer, removed a powder-blue shoulder holster holding a Beretta M9, and pulled it on under his jacket. Paul, who had been a captain in the Army Reserve, had regularly visited the firing range for years as an escape from his high-pressure job. His Beretta had been the official semi-automatic pistol used by the U.S. Armed Forces since 1985, but it needed to be updated. Paul had intended to upgrade to a later model when he learned that the Beretta would be replaced by most of the Armed Forces with a customized version of the Sig Sauer P320, which he thought he would buy instead. It wasn't lost on him that Rico used an earlier version of the Sig P320.

When he saw the look of surprise on Evelyn's face, he said, "Don't worry. I still have the permit." Then he added, "You sure?"

"Yes." Then eyeing the shoulder holster, she said, "Paul, this is a strange time to be thinking about this, but although I've seen that shoulder holster before, this is the first time I've noticed the color: powder-blue. Is that the color they usually are?"

"You know, I'm not sure."

"I just thought it was a little peculiar, that's all. Strange how the mind focuses on certain things."

"Ready?" Paul said, ignoring her comment.

Evelyn nodded.

"Let's go," he said.

Chapter Sixteen

Cleveland had seen Sadie every day since their initial meeting four days earlier, either at the drug store or her house, and once they had gone to dinner and a late movie. He had even started to loosen up a bit around her two daughters. However, he hadn't breathed a word to her about Larry or his plan to "even the score" with Rico, a plan he still fully intended to carry out.

It had been four days since Larry and Cleveland had missed Rico at his apartment. Since then they had taken turns checking in vain outside his apartment building for his car and for any lights on in his apartment. Despite telling Cleveland otherwise, Larry had never asked Gus for any leads on Rico's whereabouts, because he had no intention of letting Gus in on his plans. He knew he could never change Gus's mind about how to deal with Rico, so he decided not to try. He would wait until Rico was dead and present Gus with a fait accompli. Gus would be upset, even furious, but ultimately, he wouldn't take any punitive action against the son of his favorite sister, other than perhaps slapping him around again. Counting on that relationship had worked before and it would work again. Whether it would also work for Cleveland was not Larry's problem.

For his part, Gus assumed that Rico was recuperating in his apartment and that the incident was closed. After all, he had laid down the law and he expected his edict to be obeyed. Despite ample evidence to the contrary, he never expected from Larry the flagrant challenge to his authority that killing Rico would represent.

The same was true for Cleveland. Although technically he was outside of Gus's jurisdiction, Gus nevertheless expected him to fall in line. However, Cleveland had no intention of falling in line. Larry was right. Gus no longer ran things in the neighborhood with an iron fist. He was slipping and he'd become careless. Having no reason to suspect defiance, Gus comforted himself with two age-old maxims: "No news is good news" and "Let sleeping dogs lie."

Then Cleveland saw the newspaper. He didn't usually read the paper, but he happened to see one when he was visiting Sadie at the drug store. He was waiting for a long line of customers to clear when he casually picked it up. After glancing at the headlines, he turned the paper over and saw the story. At first, he wasn't sure, but Gabe's unusual last name had stuck in his memory when Gabe announced himself outside Rico's empty apartment. It was the same man.

Cleveland got Sadie's attention with the wave of a hand and silently mouthed, "I'll call you." She nodded and he rushed outside to call Larry. When he reached him, he said, "Man, we gotta talk. Meet me at White's Confectionary in ten minutes."

Larry was engrossed in a game of poker with three other men. "Hold on. What's so damn important? I'm in the middle of somethin' right now."

"How far away are you now?"

"Between five or ten minutes, but I told you; I'm in the middle of somethin'."

"I don't care what you're doin'. Drop it and meet me there in ten minutes."

"Wait a minute –"

Cleveland disconnected. Larry didn't call back so Cleveland assumed he got the message and would be there. He started walking. White's was about a five-minute walk away. It was a combination ice cream shop and restaurant located on Cleveland's old paper route. The place held sweet memories for him, and he became nostalgic just thinking about it. In the summertime he used to stop there almost every day on the way home to buy an ice cream cone: a double dip of butter pecan and New York Cherry. In the wintertime he dropped in at least once a week for his favorite; a bowl of steaming hot chili, sprinkled with oyster crackers.

He got there first and went inside. Mr. White, the proprietor, had died long before Cleveland left for L.A. Otherwise, the store hadn't changed much. It was located inside a compact one-story white cinder block building. There was room for only about five wooden tables, all covered with plaid tablecloths. A waiter came over and Cleveland declined his offer to see a menu and ordered a Coke. When Larry came in five minutes later, Cleveland was sipping it. The waiter approached as soon as he saw Larry, but Larry waved him away. Disappointed, the waiter retreated behind the wooden counter on the other side of the restaurant. Cleveland and Larry had the place to themselves.

Larry sat, feigning surprise and exasperation. "Well?" he said but he knew.

Cleveland didn't waste any time. "So, what the fuck happened?"

Larry was ready for the question or one like it. "I got tired of waiting so I went to his place and had a little chat with him," he said without hesitation.

"And when was I supposed to hear about this?"

"When he talked."

"Which he never did."

"You got it."

Anger boiling over, Cleveland stood, pounded his fist on the table and hovered over Larry. The waiter's eyes bulged but he said nothing.

"Man, why couldn't you just wait a few more days? I told you he was comin' back."

Larry maintained his composure. He answered calmly. "That was just a hunch. Besides, I don't like to wait."

"Did you even ask Gus?"

"No."

Cleveland shook his head. "Sometimes I wonder about you." He took a deep breath and let it out slowly. "So why did you kill the guy?"

"We went for a ride and when I stopped the car, he got out and tried to run."

"The paper said one shot, close range in the back of the head."

"I caught him."

"At his age, that must've been pretty hard to do."

"The old guy was in good shape."

"Come on, man, he had to be 75, 80 years old! That shit was un-necessary."

"So, what was I supposed to do?"

Exasperated, Cleveland sat back down, slowly sinking into his chair. "You shouldn't have snatched him in the first place. I told you I wasn't going back inside over some irrelevant shit."

"That's why I didn't bring you in the first place. So, this was me, not you."

"Yeah, but some of the stink from your shit is about to rub off on me."

Larry's irritation showed for the first time since he entered the restaurant. "Well fuck you, man, if that's the way you feel about it."

That was Cleveland's out. "And fuck you, too," he said. "I had a bad feelin' about you for a while – knockin' little boys on their ass and offin' old men for the hell of it. Shit, Sam got his ass killed for nothin!"'

The two men – Larry first – leaned across the table and inched closer to each other.

"And I had a feelin' about you, too," Larry said. "All talk. You're scared shitless about goin' back to the joint, so you're tryin' to figure a way to get the fuck back to L.A. That's why you're layin' all this shit on me."

"Tell me somethin'. You ever been inside?"

"No."

"Then shut the fuck up about bein' scared about goin' back. You *damned right* I'm scared. And I'll be goddamned if I'm goin' back because my brother – rest his stupid soul – was dumb enough to get killed over a punk-ass kid like you."

That tore it. Larry leaped to his feet and grabbed the handle of the .45 in his belt under his jacket and kept his hand there. The waiter cowered behind the counter but remained silent.

Cleveland, his hands under the table, said, "Go ahead and try me. I'll put three in you before you get that thing outta your belt. And I won't too much mind goin' back in over that."

He glared at Larry, not blinking. Larry didn't budge. The wheels were spinning in his head.

"You wanna stick your head under the table so you can see this .45 lookin' up at you?" He waited a moment, but Larry said nothing. "Put that thing on the table with your other hand."

"You're bluffin'!"

"If you think I'm bluffin', try me." Cleveland didn't break eye contact for a moment.

Larry hesitated but just for a second. As ordered, he slowly removed the gun from inside his belt and carefully placed it on the table.

"You didn't think I come in here trustin' you any farther than I could throw you, did you? Now get the fuck outta here. You can shit all over Gus's neighborhood by yourself."

Larry slunk out of the restaurant. Cleveland watched him drive away, through the open door. Then he stood, revealing the .45 in his hand, which he had deposited in his chair after he stood and pounded the table. He picked up Larry's .45 and put it in his jacket pocket, tucked his own gun in his belt, and headed for the door. On the way he realized he'd forgotten to pay for the Coke. He peeled off a five-dollar bill from his money clip, wandered over to the counter, and reached out to hand the bill to the waiter.

"No charge!" the waiter said nervously.

Cleveland smiled and turned to leave. On the way out he left the five dollars on his table.

Outside, there was no sign of Larry. '*Good*,' Cleveland said to himself. He had almost - stupidly - bought himself a one-way ticket back to prison for no good reason and, in the process, squandered a chance to settle down with a good woman. '*And for what? What the hell was I thinking?*'

He took the long way home, which meant he had to walk across a bridge spanning a river. Midway across he stopped and stood there for a little over a minute, wondering whether he should follow through with what he'd made up his mind he would do during his long trek to the bridge. He decided he should. He waited for traffic to clear in both directions. After making sure that there was no foot traffic on the bridge, he tossed both guns in the river. On the way home he called Sadie and told her he needed to talk to her, and she invited him to dinner at her house that evening.

When Cleveland arrived at Sadie's house, her two daughters greeted him at the front door and each one grabbed a hand and pulled him inside, just as they had done the last few times he'd visited. Once he was settled on the couch, competing for his attention, they brought him their dolls and asked him which one he liked better. He was still getting used to being around kids, not to mention being lavished with so much attention and affection, but he had finally stumbled on the obvious: he liked them, and they liked him.

Sadie waited patiently until after dinner to hear what Cleveland had to say. After she put the girls to bed, they retired to the living room and sat together on the couch, both facing straight ahead.

"I've got a few more things to do at the house, cleaning up, and getting rid of stuff and such, and then I'm headin' back to L.A. after the funeral," he said.

"I can help with the house if you'd like."

"That would be nice."

"I know you're still on parole and all, but I'm just surprised to hear you're leaving now – I mean so soon."

"There's nothin' left for me to do here. I got a guy to look after the house, at least until I find somebody to buy it, and –"

"I'm so happy."

Searching for the right words, Cleveland leaned forward and then back again. He finally turned to face Sadie. She turned to him and met his gaze.

"You didn't believe me, when I said I was gonna forget about what happened to Sam, did you?" he asked abruptly.

She turned away. "I'm sorry, Cleveland. I wanted to but I just wasn't sure."

He placed a finger on her cheek and gently turned her head back until she was facing him. "Don't be sorry, 'cause you were right. I looked you right in the eye and lied through my teeth. Now I'm sorry I did that to you."

"It doesn't matter, Cleveland. As long as you're being straight with me now."

"When I first got here, no way could I walk away from what happened to Sam. All I knew was my brother was dead and I didn't care how he got that way. Remember I told you about the jungle? Well, that was the jungle talkin'. But the truth is, nobody killed Sam but Sam."

"You don't have to say anything else."

"No, I want to. Today a man told me I was lookin' for excuses not to go after the man that did it. He was right and he gave me one more. But I already had three: you and those two girls of yours, Melissa and Sarah."

Overjoyed, Sadie grinned and took his hands in hers. "You really mean that, Cleveland?"

"It's only been a few days since I been back, but I think we can make a life together – if you'll have me."

"You just go on out to L.A. and stay out of trouble, and we'll be here when you get back. We might even come and visit."

Chapter Seventeen

About forty-five minutes after she left the cabin, Jean reached into her purse for her cell phone and discovered that she'd left it at the cabin. In her mind's eye she saw it immediately, lying on the coffee table where she'd accidentally left it in her mad dash to get away before Rico woke up. She hated to be without the phone; it was almost like an appendage, but she couldn't risk going back for it. Rico was probably awake by now and if not, she would undoubtedly wake him up if she tried to sneak into the cabin. She drove on.

She and Koblentz lived in the same building, on the same floor, and, in fact, her apartment was directly across from his. That proximity had allowed him to hear her screams when she was being attacked that time several months back, and to pound on her door and scare her attacker away. She had always been grateful to him, despite his own self-flagellation stemming from his hesitation in coming to her aid. He blamed himself for not getting there sooner. That was silly and she had always told him so.

Jean also told him she was grateful to him for remaining with her and comforting her until Rico could get there that night; for staying with her as needed over the next several days and helping to nurse her back to health; and for keeping her company and consoling her while Rico tracked down and ultimately dispatched her attacker.

They had not known each other well before she was attacked, but afterwards they became very close, almost like father and daughter.

Her own father had been killed in a car accident when she was a child, and Koblentz came to fill, at least somewhat, the gap in her life caused by his early death and her prolonged estrangement from her mother and three younger sisters. For his part, Koblentz had been alone for many years, ever since his wife's early death from an especially aggressive case of pneumonia that was diagnosed too late. The couple's only child, a girl, was stillborn, and he had no relatives to speak of and none at all locally. So, ironically, Jean came to fill part of an empty space in his life as well.

Jean knocked on Koblentz's door and when no one answered, she knocked again. She was about to knock a third time when a man approached from down the hall. She didn't recognize him, but he easily could have been a visitor. She knocked again and again there was no answer. By this time, the man had reached the place where she was standing. She inched closer to the door to give him a wide berth, but he didn't pass. He stopped.

"He ain't there," the man said in a gravelly voice.

Jean was wary but tried to remain calm. "Who are you?"

"A friend."

He didn't look like any friend of Gabe's that Jean had ever seen. His beady eyes stared at her menacingly and seemed to peer right through her. Stout, unshaven, and slovenly, he kept both hands buried deep in the pockets of his oversized jacket. Moreover, his appearance aside, it seemed odd to Jean that this so-called friend would be lurking in the hall if he knew Gabe was not there. "Do you know where he is or when he's coming back?" she asked.

"No, who's askin'?"

She threw his words back at him. "A friend," she said curtly.

"Listen, lady ..."

She started to back away. "That's all right. I'll try him later."

He followed. "I'll take you to him."

"No thanks." She turned and started to walk away briskly. He followed and she started to run. He caught up with her and grabbed her shoulders from behind, spinning her around. "Okay," she said and relaxed her body for a second, which caused him to let down his guard. While he continued to hold her shoulders, he loosened his grip slightly. As soon as he did, she stepped forward with her left leg, anchoring herself, and before he could react, she took aim and in one swift motion, kneed him as hard as she could in the groin with her right leg. He groaned and collapsed to his knees, clutching his crotch. She swung her purse with both hands and hit him flush on the side of his face, and he tumbled over onto the floor, causing a .45 to fall out of his pocket. Jean kicked it away and ran down the three flights of stairs to the street.

Her car was parked near the front of the building. When she reached it, she sped off and once again instinctively reached for her purse on the front seat next to her so she could retrieve her cell phone and call Rico. As her hand made contact with the purse, she remembered again that the phone wasn't there. '*Why did I pick today to forget my phone?*' she wondered, frantic. Carefully checking to make sure she wasn't being followed, she slowly drove down a few streets searching in vain for what might be the last pay phone on the planet – if she could find it. Alas, she couldn't. '*Desperate times call for desperate measures.*'

She parked the car and waited for the right candidate. He appeared three minutes later. She got out of the car and leaned against it, smoothing her hair back. A well-dressed man in his thirties wearing a three-piece suit and carrying a leather briefcase approached. When he saw Jean, he smiled broadly, admiring the view, and slowed his gait. She looked right past him at the person a few paces behind him, the person she'd spied from her car a few moments earlier; a boy of about fifteen wearing jeans and a T-shirt and holding a phone to his ear.

She waved an arm to get the boy's attention. When he looked in her direction, she said, "Excuse me, young man, can I talk to you for a second?"

Flabbergasted, he stopped, pointed a finger to his chest, and mouthed, "Me?"

"Yes, you," she said, gifting him with a warm smile.

"I have to call you back," he said into the phone and wandered over and stood in front of her. "Hi," he said shyly.

"How are you?"

"Fine, I guess."

"Good. Listen, how would you like to make ten dollars?"

"How?"

"Just let me borrow your phone for a minute. I forgot mine and I have to make a *really* important call. How about it?"

"I don't know…"

"Wait a minute." She leaned into the car and got the keys and her purse. She took out a ten-dollar bill from her wallet. "Hold your hand out."

He slowly extended his hand, palm open. She put the ten dollars and her car keys in his hand. "See," she said. "I'm not going anywhere because you have my keys. Okay now?"

The boy tugged at his ear uncertainly and rubbed his chin. "Take it," he said. "But just for a minute."

She smiled and he handed her the phone. "I'll be right over here," she said and moving a few steps away, swiftly punched in Rico's number. He answered immediately.

When she'd finished explaining what had happened, Rico said, "Okay, take a deep breath. You did good. The worst is over now."

"Rico, do you think he's okay? I mean, they could be holding him somewhere or…"

"Listen, I gotta tell you somethin' and I want you to try to hold it together, okay?"

She held her breath. "Go ahead."

"They got to him. One shot to the back of the head."

Jean closed her eyes. "Oh, God. I guess I knew." She struggled to hold them back, but a single tear trickled down her cheek. She wiped it away. "But why him? He never hurt anyone in his life."

"Maybe not, but he was a tough old bird. He didn't talk."

"How could he? He didn't know where we were."

"He knew how to get you on the phone, and I know they asked."

"Poor, sweet Gabe... Rico, how did you know that he was... I mean, how did you find out?"

"Your friend, the lawyer. It was in the papers. I'm standin' on the porch...." He eased into a chair and emitted a sigh of relief. "...Make that sittin' on the porch, keepin' a lookout for him now."

"But –"

"We can talk about that later. Right now, we gotta get you off the street. I want you to go to Buster's Café. I'll call him from here. He'll hide you out until I get back to the city."

"Okay. I'll go now. Anything else?"

"Just make sure that asshole whose voice you just made a couple of pitches higher is not followin' you."

Jean, in a daze, walked slowly back to where the boy stood waiting. As she neared him, she wiped another tear from her eye. "Thanks for the use of the phone," she said and handed it to him.

He took the phone and handed the keys back to Jean. "You okay, lady?"

"I'm fine," she said and smiled sadly.

The boy tugged at his ear and rubbed his chin once more. "Here, lady," he said and extended a hand holding the ten dollars.

"No, that's for you," Jean insisted, her mood brightening a little. "I really needed to make that call. If you hadn't loaned me your phone, I don't know what I would have done. So, I want you to have it."

"Okay," he said. "I hope everything works out for you."

"Thanks," she said and leaned in and kissed him on the cheek. He didn't say a word, just grinned from ear to ear, his cheeks glowing pink.

Chapter Eighteen

When Paul and Evelyn arrived at his cabin, they saw Rico sitting lazily in one of the chairs on the porch, patiently awaiting their arrival. The weather was warm and windy and the leafy layers of trees surrounding the cabin swayed softly in the breeze. A dozen sparrows alighted from the road in front of the approaching car and frantically flapped their wings as they hurriedly took flight to avoid its tires.

As the car got closer, Rico noticed Evelyn sitting in the front seat, her eyes locked on him. Her gaze was hot with anger. His was cool, dispassionate. After the car came to a stop, Paul got out and came over to the cabin while Evelyn waited in the car.

"Ready?" Paul asked, dispensing with small talk.

"Let's do it," Rico said. "I already locked the door. I cleared our things; do me a favor and grab that bag."

"Sure."

Rico had his cane but didn't deign to use it. He carried it instead and limped to the passenger side of the car. When they reached it, Rico handed Paul the key to the cabin. There then ensued an awkward moment of silence, which was broken by Paul's perfunctory introduction.

"Evelyn, this is Richard Sanders."

"Make it 'Rico'," Rico said.

"Rico, this is Evelyn."

"McDuffie," Rico said.

"No, Rogers," Evelyn said icily. "I use my maiden name since my husband's death."

"I should have known that," Rico said.

"Yes, you should have," Evelyn said.

Paul deposited Rico's bag in the trunk, walked around the front of the car, and got in behind the wheel while Rico sat in the back seat, behind Evelyn. There followed more awkward silence for the next several miles until Rico broke it with a question for Paul. "So, what kind of law do you practice, counselor?"

"Civil."

"I kinda figured that, big firm and all. Litigation, corporate, IP…?"

"IP? You know what that is?" Paul asked.

"I didn't just crawl out from under a rock. Intellectual property, if I'm not mistaken."

"You aren't."

"So, which is it?" Rico asked.

"Litigation," Paul answered, glancing in the rear-view mirror at Rico.

"Litigator or trial lawyer? I hear some lawyers think there's a difference."

"Some do," Paul agreed.

"I figure you for a trial lawyer."

"Perspicacious of you."

"You've been talking to Jean. But, of course, I knew that."

Evelyn sighed audibly. Her attitude – ignoring Rico but doing so with a passion – amused him. He smiled to himself.

"Do you mind if we listen to some music, Mr. Sanders?" she asked.

"Rico," he corrected her.

"Do you mind?" she repeated coldly.

"No."

"Do you know anything about jazz, Mr. Sanders?"

"Rico," he corrected her again.

Evelyn turned to face him. "Do you?"

"A little," Rico said.

"As much as you know about lawyers?"

"About."

"What do you like?"

"Straight ahead, mostly. And mostly the older players. Some Bebop, Coleman Hawkins, Lester Young, Bird, Dexter Gordon, Mingus, Miles, of course… that doesn't include any vocalists, but I could name a few."

"Eclectic tastes for a man in the business of…"

"Whatever it is, it doesn't make me brain dead." He cocked an eyebrow at her.

There was a long moment of silence as Evelyn tried to think of a come-back. When she couldn't do so immediately, she started to turn back around when she noticed that Rico's coat jacket was open just enough for her to see part of his powder-blue shoulder holster. She hesitated, frozen in her seat. "Same color!" she said under her breath.

"Come again?" Rico said.

"Nothing," Evelyn said. "I was just about to say I can't figure you out."

"I wouldn't let it bother you. Not only is the night still young, it's not even sundown yet."

It was true. She couldn't figure him out. He was a professional killer. That much was clear but not much else was. He'd killed her lying, cheating, and thieving husband and her erstwhile girlfriend who had been having an affair with him, right under her nose. It didn't matter that she had already decided to divorce him. Neither of them deserved to be assassinated by a cold-blooded killer, the same cold-blooded killer who had come close to killing her and Paul because he thought they were in possession of the pigeon-blood red ruby necklace that her husband had stolen.

But then, completely against expectations, the very same killer had spared her life and Paul's after Paul, through a twist of fate, had saved his. She was torn between resentment and relief.

No, she couldn't figure Rico out. Even before today she'd thought he was a ball of contradictions. Now, meeting him for the first time, he seemed to her to be intelligent, even witty. And that was the problem. Those qualities, she believed, along with Rico's darker side, held some kind of fascination for Paul, because, consciously or subconsciously, some part of Paul wanted to emulate Rico. '*Becoming comfortable carrying a gun at all was bad enough, but even if subconsciously, Paul had gone out and bought a shoulder holster that was the same unusual color as the one Rico wore. Surely, powder-blue shoulder holsters were not that common. Paul was a lawyer, for heaven sake! What was he doing wearing a powder-blue shoulder holster?*'

She knew she was acting like a shrew but so be it. She refused to be seduced by Rico's charm the way Paul seemed to be, and she would do everything in her power to keep Paul from acting out whatever boyhood fantasy that was causing him to draw closer to this killer.

For his part, Paul listened in silence while Evelyn tried to put Rico in his place. He understood what she was doing and why. She had told him often enough. But he was certain that she really didn't have anything to worry about. He was not in danger of becoming another Rico or anything close. True, despite logic and reason, some part of him couldn't help admiring the man. He had saved his life and Evelyn's, despite previously being on the verge of taking them. Now he went out of his way to protect Paul, despite Paul's protestations. Paul was convinced that that kind of fealty demanded something from him in return. He told himself that not everything in life fits neatly in its proper place. Rico was a conundrum, but he'd made peace with the situation. What remained to be done was to bring Evelyn around.

After Cleveland threw him out of the restaurant, it took every ounce of the little self-control that Larry possessed to keep him from rushing home, picking up one of his spare guns and hunting Cleveland down. He forced himself to wait, though, because he had something better in mind.

He pulled over to the curb and parked his car. Then he punched in a number on his cell phone. After a short exchange with the person on the other end, he asked, "Okay, who can I get to do this?" The person gave him a name and Larry said, "Ralph. All right. Give me his number."

After he got the number, he punched it in on his cell. There followed another brief conversation, at the end of which Larry said, "Okay, there's a grand in it for you. Wait outside until I come and get you."

Before Cleveland called him, Larry had planned to break the news to Gus about Koblentz after he finished his poker game, but now was the perfect time. On the way to Gus's house, he stopped at a convenience store to buy a newspaper.

It turned out that the newspaper wasn't necessary. Gus was holding one when he greeted Larry at his front door. "Come in," Gus said, his voice betraying no emotion. "Have a seat." Larry was silent. He took a seat across from Gus, who sat in his recliner holding the newspaper in his lap. Gus looked down at the newspaper and back up at Larry. "You wanna explain this?" he asked evenly.

"I brought one in case you hadn't seen it," Larry said, holding his newspaper up for Gus to see.

"So, tell me. What happened?"

"One word: Cleveland."

"The hell he did!" Gus said incredulously.

"I didn't believe it either."

"When did you find out about this?"

"I was there."

"And why did I have to find out about it in this piece of shit paper?" Gus asked, his anger rising. Before Larry could answer, Gus threw the newspaper on the floor.

"I shoulda told you."

"I know you shoulda told me. Why didn't you?"

"'Cause it was partially my fault. I shoulda handled it and I didn't."

Gus shook his head, trying to calm down. "What the hell happened?"

"Cleveland and me was cruisin' down the street when I recognized the old guy walking toward us. I just casually mentioned it to Cleveland, and he told me to pull over. He said he wanted to talk to the guy. I said it was a bad idea, but he wanted to stop, so I did."

Still trying to keep his anger in check, Gus bent down, picked up the paper, folded it neatly, and put it in his lap. "That was your first mistake."

"Next thing I know Cleveland's got him in the back seat givin' him the third degree, you know. 'Where's Rico? Where's his girlfriend? You gotta know his cell number or hers. Call one of 'em or I'm gonna beat the shit outta you.' On and on like that."

"Let me guess," Gus said sarcastically. "He didn't talk."

"The old guy had balls. He didn't say a word."

Gus let out a deep sigh and shook his head again. "Okay, get to the end. How did it go down?"

"We took him to the edge of town. I thought we was gonna let him go. And all of a sudden, Cleveland went off on him, you know. Like somethin' snapped. I tried to stop him but before I could get to him, it was all over."

Gus continued to shake his head. "Stupid, stupid shit. Why didn't you at least make sure the body stayed at the bottom of the river?"

"Ask Cleveland," Larry said sheepishly.

"I'm askin' you."

"I think he wanted the body to be found. To smoke Rico out."

"Didn't you help him?"

"No. We put the body in the trunk. I was so pissed off, I gave him the keys and told him to get rid of it."

Deep in thought, Gus lowered his eyes, clasped his fingers under his chin, and slowly shook his head. After a moment, he looked up and said, "Larry, I gotta hand it to you. You almost had me."

Larry sprang to his feet and stood facing Gus. "What? You think I'm shittin' you?"

Gus lost it. He stood, took one step forward, and grasped Larry by the throat with both hands. He started to strangle him. "You damned right, I do!"

Gasping for air, Larry grabbed Gus's wrists and tried in vain to loosen his grip. He managed to say, "I swear to you, Gus. That's the way it went down!"

Little by little, Gus released his grip on Larry's throat and slowly sank into his chair. Exasperated, he looked up and said, "What the fuck am I gonna do with you, Larry?"

Still recovering, Larry bent forward, gasping, his hands pressing against his thighs. "Dammit, Gus! I can prove it!"

Gus just stared at him as he turned and stumbled out of the house, leaving the front door open. A moment later he came back inside with another short and stocky man about Cleveland's age in tow. He slammed the door behind him.

"What the hell is this?" Gus asked.

"I was with him when Cleveland told him what happened," Larry said.

"Is that right?" Gus asked.

"Yeah, that's right," the man said.

"Who the hell are you?" Gus asked.

"I used to hang around with Cleveland before he moved to LA. Him and Larry stopped by my place and had a beer later that night after Cleveland shot that guy."

"He told you he shot him?"

"Yeah. He told me he shot him and dumped him in the lake. He was real upset. Said the guy was jerkin' him around."

Gus was not convinced. "And what did Larry say?"

"He didn't say too much of nothin'. He was just lettin' Cleveland blow off some steam and settle down, that's all."

"You sure you tellin' this to me straight?" Gus pressed.

"I'm just tellin' you what Cleveland said. That's pretty much all of it."

Gus was still skeptical. "You know Larry here?" Gus asked.

"I just met him when Cleveland brought him by my place."

"Well, how did he get in touch with you today?"

"He stopped by and asked me to meet him here, but he asked me to wait outside."

"He give you anything?" Gus asked.

"Not a dime. He just said you might not believe him, and you wanted to know the truth. I know Cleveland from way back and I don't wanna get him in trouble or nothin', but he wasn't tryin' to hide what he did. Listen, I wouldn't tell the cops if they asked, but I know you, I mean I know who you are and your reputation and all, and I don't wanna get crosswise with you."

Gus stared hard at the man, trying to size him up. Then he made up his mind. He'd heard enough. "What's your name, anyway?"

"Ralph."

"Okay, Ralph, you can go."

"That's it?" Ralph asked.

"Yeah, that's it," Gus said.

Ralph headed for the door, and Larry patted hm on the back as he left and came back and stood silently in front of Gus.

Gus leaned forward in his chair. "I must be slippin'," he said. "I really read Cleveland wrong." Then he sighed and rubbed his chin, once again deep in thought. "It may not be too late. It might work."

"What?" Larry said.

Gus didn't answer. He stood and said, "Let's go."

They took Larry's car. Once inside, Gus continued to keep Larry in the dark and Larry waited patiently. For him, the worst was over. He'd laid the blame for Koblentz's death on Cleveland and Gus had clearly swallowed it. But Gus was still peeved at Larry, just not as much as he'd been before Ralph confirmed Larry's story.

"Where to?" Larry asked.

"Just drive."

"Yeah, but which way?"

"Just drive."

After a couple of minutes, Gus took out his cell phone and punched in some numbers. The bartender answered. "Do me a favor," Gus said. "Call Cleveland's house. You already got the number. If he's there, tell him you got somebody at the bar who wants to buy the house. If he's not there, try his cell." He turned to Larry. "Give him the number."

Gus handed his cell to Larry. Larry gave the bartender the number and handed the phone back to Gus.

"Okay," the bartender said after a moment. "I got it. What's the guy's name?"

"There is no guy. Just make somethin' up. Tell him the guy wants to stop by to take a real quick look at the place. And it's gotta be in the next few minutes because the guy is leavin' town. Then call me back on my cell. You got that?"

"Got it."

"So, what's gonna happen if we get him there," Larry asked.

"Let me worry about that," Gus said, still peeved. "Just start drivin' in that direction."

After they had driven a few minutes, the bartender called back. "He can't make it until this evening. Somethin' about a woman he's seein'."

"Okay," Gus said. "Tell him the guy will have to pull some strings, but he can wait. He'll stop by later."

"Well?" Larry said.

"Cleveland can't get there until this evening. We'll swing around later."

Chapter Nineteen

As Paul's car approached the city, Rico said, "Drop me off at a joint called 'Buster's Café. You know it?"

"Yes."

"I'm shocked."

"I grew up near there," Paul said.

"Shocked again. We coulda been neighbors. You moved out and I stayed."

"Ironic."

"What did your ol' man do?" Rico asked.

"Auto mechanic. He passed away a couple of years ago. Had a heart attack. Yours?"

"Worked in the steel mill but he always wanted to be an English teacher. Surprised?"

"A little."

"Is that how you learned all those big words – that you only use with Jean?"

"We talked a lot."

"Still alive?"

"Hardly."

"What happened to him?"

"Not important."

"I'm curious," Paul said. "How long have you been with Jean?"

"A few years."

"I was telling Evelyn she seems like a special person."

"She is."

Evelyn turned around to face Rico. "I'd like to meet her."

Rico's face wore a puzzled look. "Shocked again."

"Does that mean you'll introduce her to me?"

"If everything is okay, you can meet her at Buster's."

Paul's ears perked up. "What do you mean, 'If everything's okay?' "

"Somebody tried to get to me through her. She was outside Gabe Koblentz's apartment when it happened."

"Is she all right?" Evelyn asked.

"She's a tough cookie," Rico said. Then he said to Paul, "When we get there, let me off in front and drive around the block a couple of times. If it's safe, I'll wave you in." Turning back to Evelyn, he asked, "Still wanna see her?"

"Yes."

Larry dropped Gus off at his house, and Gus told him to drive straight home and wait until Gus called. No exceptions. Gus went inside and slumped into his recliner. His wife heard the door open and came into the living room from her bedroom. She was a thin woman – almost emaciated – with steel gray hair and inquisitive, bright blue eyes. She immediately noticed the weary look on Gus's face. "Is everything all right?"

"Just business," he said.

She knew that was a discussion ender, just as it would have been had Rico given the same answer to Jean. "Oh," she said and let the matter drop.

They had been married for thirty years, and she knew exactly what he meant by "business." She used to worry and tie herself into knots whenever he left the house, as there was a fair chance that the next time she saw him he'd either be in the hospital, in jail, or in the morgue.

"I could eat somethin'," Gus said offhandedly.

There was left-over roast beef in the refrigerator. "Roast beef sandwich okay?" She was up and on her way to the kitchen before he could answer, and as she reached the doorway, she turned for his response. He nodded.

While his wife was in the kitchen, Gus made a call. When the person on the other end answered, Gus said, "Did you get the car?" He waited for a response and said, "What color is it?" He waited again until he got the answer and said, "Okay, got it. Bring it around and park it a few houses down the street from me."

After Gus ate, they watched TV for a few hours until Gus grew sleepy. He decided to take a nap in his recliner and asked his wife to wake him in an hour, which she dutifully did. Once awakened, he called the bartender again and asked him to check to see if Cleveland was at his house. The bartender called and reported to Gus that he was there. Gus rose to leave and, uncharacteristically, his wife walked him to the door.

"This shouldn't take too long," he said.

"All right, I'll wait up for you."

"No need for that," Gus said. "I might stop at the bar afterwards."

"No, I'll wait up," she said. "And Gus, be careful, okay?"

Her words surprised him. It was a casual thing to say, but she hadn't said it in a long time. "Sure," he said and gave her a peck on the cheek.

As she watched him through the window, she brought a hand to the cheek he'd kissed and held it there until he was out of sight.

Gus picked up the car that had been dropped off for him. Once he was on the way to Larry's house, he called Larry and told him to meet him outside in ten minutes. When he pulled up to Larry's house, Larry was waiting outside on the tree lawn. He examined the car. "Where did this come from?" he asked.

"One of the guys boosted it for me," Gus said. "You got your piece?"

Larry smiled and opened his jacket, revealing his Glock tucked under his belt.

"Get in," Gus said.

They drove to Cleveland's house in silence. As they turned on to Cleveland's street, Larry started to say something, but Gus cut him off. "I don't wanna hear it. Just be ready. I'll park a couple of houses away and leave the keys in the car. You go in the front but give me a couple of minutes to walk around back to block that door before you ring the doorbell. All we need is for him to try to run. As soon as he opens the door, let him have it. Then drive around and pick me up in the alley. One, two, three. Got it?"

Larry nodded and screwed up his courage. He was good at knocking kids on their asses and slapping around women and old men – not so good at taking on someone his own size, face to face. If Cleveland came to the door carrying a gun, he wasn't sure he could get the drop on him. And the door had a peep hole. What if he couldn't coax Cleveland into opening it? Gus had made it clear that he didn't want to discuss it and he expected Larry to do whatever was necessary to get the job done. So he was silent and hoped for the best.

As the car neared the house, they got a surprise. Cleveland was out front carrying two large trash bags toward the curb. Gus pulled up and stopped the car in front of his house. He left the motor running.

Cleveland saw Gus and Larry and approached the car warily. "What do you want?" he asked just before he reached the passenger side of the car. "I told Larry…"

"Now!" Gus shouted.

Instinctively, Cleveland tried to shield himself behind the trash bags, which he hoisted in front of him. Sadie, who had been watching from an upstairs window, sensed what was playing out in front of her and screamed just as Larry fired four shots. "Cleveland, Cleveland, no, no, no …!"

Hearing the scream, Gus floored the accelerator, burning rubber, and sped away. Sadie rushed down the stairs, out the door, and across the lawn to where Cleveland lay sprawled on the tree lawn and cradled him in her arms. "Sometimes… sometimes you live in the jungle for so long, you can't… you just can't get out," Cleveland said, struggling to talk.

"No, you did get out," Sadie said, crying. "No matter what happens, Cleveland, you got out. You hear me, Cleveland? You got out.…"

Chapter Twenty

Rico and Buster Kincaid went back a long way. He was Rico's father's best friend. Nobody knew how Rico's father died except Rico, because only he was there when it happened, and he told no one. But, being so close to Rico's father, Buster had an inkling of what took place. He was one of a handful of people who knew about the father's dream to become an English teacher and to leave his job in the steel mill where he and Buster had worked side by side until just before Rico's father's death.

Buster had a modest dream of his own, which was to open the small business that became Buster's Café. Rico's father never realized his dream, but his death was the catalyst that enabled Buster to finally realize his.

There was another link between Rico and Buster, beyond Buster's friendship with Rico's father. Some five years earlier Buster was being harassed by a couple of thugs who regularly robbed his store and demanded protection money to stop. He refused and bought a gun. The next time they showed up demanding money, Buster brandished the gun and they backed down. However, he had received only the briefest of reprieves. The two men came back later that night with reinforcements: two other men. All four men were heavily armed. Buster was a shopkeeper, not a gunman. He did the only thing he could. He threw up his hands. And while one of them acted as lookout, the other three administered a beating he would not soon forget.

That was when Buster called Rico. The two had kept in contact since Rico's father died, and Rico regularly patronized Buster's store. Buster did the bulk of the talking, largely reminiscing about Rico's father and the old days working at the steel mill. Mostly, Rico listened.

Buster didn't know how Rico earned his living, but he had his suspicions, which Rico would have confirmed if he'd asked, but he never did and Rico, being Rico, never volunteered. Buster was a proud man, which is why he waited so long to contact Rico, and when he finally did, he only asked for advice. Rico's laconic response was, "Let me see what I can do."

Rico knew all of the crime bosses in town and they all knew him or, if not, they knew about him. In fact, many of them had used his services at one time or another. Rico made some calls and found out that the men who had put the squeeze on Buster had been on a lark of their own and that nothing had been sanctioned by any of the bosses. The men were trying to make some money on the side, under the table, so to speak. This was a no-no. If anyone made any money in any boss's territory, he expected his cut, no matter how small. Not to mention, there was the principle of the thing. No illicit activity happened in any territory that a boss didn't sanction. The thugs who hassled Buster knew that, but they thought if they limited their activities to a few small-time businesses, they would not be found out. And if Rico hadn't become involved, they may have been right.

When the bosses found out about the men shaking Buster down, they were not happy. That kind of transgression could have earned them a death sentence, but the bosses were lenient. Instead, they gave the men who had accosted Buster some of their own medicine. They had a few men administer the same kind of beating to the four transgressors they had dished out to Buster, i.e., one they wouldn't soon forget. They got the message. And that was the last Buster heard from them.

But it wasn't the last Rico heard. He hadn't made any secret of the fact that he was the one who blew the whistle on the men in question. Once again, being Rico, he really didn't care whether they found out or not. That stoical attitude was part of his persona. It was who he was, and it was one of the reasons he had the kind of reputation he did.

Soon the grapevine worked, and the men found out who had revealed their little scheme.

And Rico found out that they had found out.

He didn't know for sure what they would do, but he assumed they would come after him sooner or later. The bosses told them to lay off Buster, but they didn't say anything about Rico. And he knew it. When he wasn't working for one of them, he was on his own. And he knew that, too.

If they did come after him, of course, they would also be running the risk that Rico would make them pay a second time. But Rico figured they would likely calculate that the risk was slight, considering their four-to-one advantage. In theory, they would be right. But this wasn't theory.

If they didn't already know who they were dealing with, Rico knew that by now they would have asked around and found out. One of them did know but the other three, like Larry, were skeptical. So, they asked. What they learned would have deterred most men, but there were two kinds of men who, under the circumstances, refuse to be deterred: men who were too dumb to appreciate the danger they faced and men who were too foolhardy to care. Rico figured there was a good chance these men were both dumb and foolhardy; since they were dumb and foolhardy enough to cross the boss, they were probably dumb and foolhardy enough to come after him.

And he wasn't wrong.

In those days Jerry was still alive. Whenever Rico needed backup or an extra set of eyes, Jerry had been the guy he called. He had been the closest thing to a good friend Rico had, and although he didn't like to admit it, from time to time, Rico missed him. Jerry could hold his own, but he was outclassed by Rico in every way: intellect, physical dexterity, and raw strength. It had often bothered Jerry and although he kept it inside, Rico knew and, again, being Rico, he hadn't gone out of his way to make it easy for Jerry. Sometimes he wished he had.

This being personal, Rico didn't want Jerry to get caught in the crossfire between him and the men he suspected might come out of the woodwork at any time, but he figured he would have enough leeway to deal with that when the time came.

It took only three days.

Rico and Jerry had just finished a routine job: collecting a wad of cash from someone who owed one of the bosses a huge gambling debt. The man had the money and didn't offer any resistance. Anticipating Rico and Jerry's visit, he'd borrowed the money from a loan shark, a classic case of borrowing from Peter to pay Paul. If he got lucky, he might have the money to pay off that debt when it came due. If not, he could expect another visit from another version of Rico and Jerry.

It was after midnight and the one-way street that fronted the man's apartment building was all but deserted, save for parked cars on both sides, including Rico's car, which was parked about twenty yards from the entrance to the apartment building. Rico stepped out on to the side-walk first. The nearest streetlight was only about thirty yards away, but it was antiquated and emitted little more than a dull, yellow glow. Therefore, when Rico looked in both directions before heading to his car, he could just make out the silhouetted forms of two men seated low in the front seat of one car several cars ahead of his and two men similarly seated in the front seat of another car several cars behind his. Both cars were parked on the same side of the street as his and were pointing in the same direction.

As the men were sitting unnaturally low in their seats, he could see only the tops of their heads. However, when Jerry checked in both directions, he could only make out the top of the head of one of the two men in the car behind Rico's. He thought the man was probably asleep. But Rico knew otherwise. It was time get Jerry out of the way. He whispered to him, "See those four guys?"

"I see one," Jerry said.

"There's one more in that car and two in another car ahead. You see them?"

130

Jerry looked again and strained hard until he saw the heads of all four men. "Yeah, I see now. What of it?"

"I'm expectin' a visit from at least four guys. This may be them. It's not business. It's personal. You hang back here while I check it out."

"Wait a minute," Jerry said. "Lemme help."

"I know you wanna help, but just hang back here and keep your eye on the car up ahead. If I play this wrong, there's no need for both of us to get shot to hell."

Jerry knew it wouldn't do any good to protest further, so he watched and waited while Rico strolled back toward the car behind his. Suddenly, the car in front sped off, burning rubber. Rico kept walking and quickened his pace. Jerry stayed put.

The men in the other car saw Rico approaching and in unison slowly sat up straight in their seats. Then, the driver lost his nerve. He hurriedly started the car, jerked it into reverse and slammed into the car behind him. The passenger, a sawed-off shotgun in his lap, looked on in horror and yelled, "Jesus!" Quickly the driver shifted into gear and floored the pedal but that just caused the car to stall. By then, Rico, his Sig Sauer now in his hand, was twenty feet away and closing fast.

Holding his shotgun, the passenger hastily jumped out of the car. Instead of crouching behind it for cover and taking aim from there, he foolishly stood, ramrod straight, and leveled the shotgun at Rico. Before he could pull the trigger, he was already falling to the pavement, and he was dead before he landed. Rico had shot him once through the forehead and once through the heart for good measure without slowing his pace.

Meanwhile, the panicky driver abandoned his efforts to start the car and, following the lead of the unfortunate passenger, leaped out on to the tree lawn next to the car. Unlike his accomplice, though, he prudently took cover behind the car door. Unfortunately, his .45 was still in his shoulder holster and he fumbled desperately to get it out. When, finally, he freed the weapon, he quickly rested its barrel on the bottom edge of the open window and peered out through the window frame to get a bead on Rico. But Rico was nowhere in sight. He was already standing next to the driver, his Sig still at his side.

The barrel of the driver's weapon was still resting on the bottom edge of the window frame pointing in the direction from whence Rico had come. At last, the driver turned to his left and looked up at Rico, terror in his eyes. "Take your best shot," Rico said in a low growl. The man rose from his crouching position and pivoted to face Rico, swinging his gun hand around as he did. Just before the weapon reached the end of its arc, Rico jerked his arm upward and, without pausing to take aim, fired once. The man released his weapon and it dropped to the ground an instant before he did. Rico had shot him neatly between the eyes.

Holding his .45 in the air, Jerry came running to join Rico, but Rico waved him off and trotted toward him. By now the lights in a smattering of apartments on both sides of the street had come on. "Let's go before we wake up the whole goddamn neighborhood," Rico said.

Just then the car that had sped away rounded the corner a hundred yards behind them and came barreling down the street toward them. The driver hadn't fled the scene; he had only gone around the block and now was back, but the front seat passenger had moved to the back seat behind the driver, from which vantage point he could shoot directly at Rico and Jerry without having to fire across the car past the driver.

Both the driver and his passenger were holding .45's, and they started shooting as the car got within range of Rico and Jerry. "Get down!" Rico yelled, and they took cover behind a parked car. "Amateurs," Rico said through clenched teeth. "Neither one of them can hit shit with a .45 moving that fast, especially the driver. He'll wreck the damn car if we don't kill him first."

The speeding car, as if on cue, screeched to a stop. "I guess they heard you," Jerry said.

The two men kept firing, but Rico and Jerry were well protected by the car between them and the gunmen. "Try for the guy in the back seat," Rico said. "I'll go for the driver." Jerry nodded and Rico duckwalked toward the front of the car while Jerry crawled toward the back. They waited. After a few seconds they heard the distinctive 'click' sound as the shooter in the back seat released a clip and started to load another. "Now!" Rico shouted. Jerry took aim and fired four times, hitting his target in the neck and chest.

The driver was still firing when Rico saw an opening and took it. The driver had momentarily turned his head and glanced backward after Jerry shot his partner, and in that instant Rico fired once, hitting him in the side of the head. He fell forward and sideways, and his body bounced off the steering wheel on to the passenger seat, but the weight of his body caused his foot to press on the gas pedal before falling away. The car lurched forward then sideways, before finally crashing into a parked car on the opposite side of the street.

More lights came on here and there in apartments up and down the street. Rico and Jerry scrambled to their car trying to beat the policemen who surely had been summoned by numerous 911 calls. The car containing the dead bodies of the two shooters was blocking their path, so Rico had to back down the street to the nearest intersection. As his car got to within one hundred feet of the intersection, a car that had been slowly coming toward them suddenly stopped and blocked their way. All they could see at first were its headlights. "Well, at least it's not the cops," Jerry said.

Rico donned his ever-present sunglasses and got out of the car. He could see just about as well wearing them in the dark as he could without them. "Get behind the wheel and keep backing up," Rico said. The car blew its horn and the driver stuck his head out of the window. "Can't you see this is a one-way street?" he said.

"Can't you see I'm backin' up?" Rico retorted, brandishing his Sig. The man's eyes bulged, and his jaw dropped. Rico said, "Now *you* back up."

The car didn't move. Something wasn't right. Rico kept walking. When he reached the front of the car, the man stuck his arm out of the window. He was holding a .45. "Shit," Rico said under his breath.

The man said nothing. Rico looked into his eyes and saw trepidation and indecision.

He took a chance.

He lunged for the man's arm and grabbed it. Then he twisted his wrist until he dropped the weapon. He reached into the car with both hands, took hold of the man by his collar, and yanked him halfway out through the window. He was a scrawny teenager, about eighteen or nineteen.

"What the hell?" Rico said when he got a good look at the youth. "You with those assholes?" he asked, twisting his head in the direction of the two dead men.

"One of 'em's my cousin," the boy yelped, and Rico shoved him back in the window.

"Jesus Christ," Rico said, shaking his head. "You coulda ended up just like them." He picked up the .45 from the ground and got behind the wheel while the kid, scared to death, scooted across into the passenger seat. Rico rapidly backed the car across the intersection and parked it. Then he jumped out and took the .45 and the keys with him.

"As far as I'm concerned, this is over," Rico said. "You had your chance back there and you didn't take it. I won't give you another one. I don't kill kids. But if it's me or you, it damn sure won't be me. Understand?" The kid nodded, eyes wide. "I wanna hear you say it," Rico said. "Are we done?"

"Yeah, we're done."

Rico hoped so.

Jerry quickly backed the car up to where Rico had parked the other car. Rico got in and Jerry drove away. Careful not to speed, they listened for police sirens. "What was that all about?" Jerry asked.

"Damn fool kid," was all Rico said.

They were lucky. They didn't hear any police sirens until they were blocks away. Once they were in the clear, Rico turned to Jerry. "You did okay back there." It was a rare compliment coming from him.

Jerry smiled. "Yeah, I guess I did."

Chapter Twenty-One

Paul pulled up outside Buster's Café and nosed the car into a parking spot near the entrance. The café featured floor-to-ceiling windows with no shades or curtains and an uncovered glass door. The lights were on but, besides Buster, the place appeared to be empty.

"Remember, when you circle back, if there's any sign of trouble, just keep drivin'," Rico said. It was early evening and the sun had begun to set on the horizon. Still, Rico donned his sunglasses before he got out of the car, leaving his cane behind. Paul acknowledged him with a nod and drove off.

Rico limped in and closed the door behind him. Buster, squat and broad-shouldered, stood behind a glass counter stocked with pies, cakes, and pastries. Before they could greet each other, the door opened behind Rico. He had a decision to make before the door closed because by then, he could be dead.

He thought whoever was behind him could be any one of three persons: he could be the man who had accosted Jean (or someone working with him); he could be a person or persons with Jean in tow, possibly holding a gun to her head; or he could be a customer.

If the first option turned out to be true, he calculated the chances were greater than not that he would already have been shot, and obviously he was still standing.

If the second option were true, to free Jean, he would have to make a sudden move for the assailant's gun or his own, either of which could get her or him, or both of them killed. He figured the chances were less than fifty per cent that Jean was behind him, mainly because, even with his back turned and several feet separating them, he was pretty sure he would have detected the scent of her perfume, and he hadn't.

Therefore, his gut told him the third option was the most likely to be true. But as soon as he reached that conclusion, he realized hearing the door open had caused him to forget to study Buster's face for clues. His eyes quickly shifted his gaze to the face in front of him for the slightest hint of apprehension. It was completely inscrutable.

The door closed behind Rico.

Buster looked past Rico, and said, "Hello, Mrs. Kellogg. Nice to see you." But his face remained impossible to read.

Rico hung back and kept his eyes on the door. He wasn't about to have it open behind him again. Mrs. Kellogg bought two apple pies to go and smiled at Rico as she exited.

"Everything okay?" Rico asked as he cautiously approached the counter.

"Sure," Buster said. "Jean's in the back room." But now his face wore a worried, agitated look. Rico noticed.

The bottom of the glass counter ended approximately two feet above the floor. There was an almost imperceptible movement of a shadow on the floor next to where Buster was standing. Rico noticed that, too.

He unholstered his Sig, quickly screwed a silencer onto the barrel, and continued moving warily toward the counter, pointing the .45 directly ahead. "How about a piece of cherry pie, then?"

The man who had attacked Jean rose from the floor behind the counter, gun drawn and pointed at Rico. Before he could pull the trigger, Rico shot him once in the forehead. The man's knees buckled, and he tilted sideways toward Buster, who scampered out of the way.

Buster mopped his brow with the back of his hand and let out a gusty breath. "He's alone," Buster said, anticipating Rico's question. "He's got Jean tied and gagged in the back room, but she's okay. I'm sorry I couldn't warn you when you first came in. I was afraid Mrs. Kellogg might read something on my face and make this guy think I was trying to warn you."

"Don't worry," Rico said. "You did all right."

He went to a door on the other side of the café, slowly opened it, and stepped inside. Jean was sitting on the floor with her mouth gagged, her back against the wall, her arms tied behind her, and her legs tied at the ankles. Rico gently removed the gag from her mouth. "You okay?"

"I'm sorry, Rico. I could have gotten us both killed."

"Is that the same guy from Koblentz's place?"

"Yeah. I guess I did a piss-poor job of losing him."

"That's okay. Dust yourself off and powder your nose. Somebody wants to meet you."

"What?"

"I'll explain later." Rico cut away her bonds and helped her to her feet. Jean rolled her shoulders and stamped her feet to get the blood circulating again after her cramped time on the floor.

Buster came over and poked his head in the room. Now Rico anticipated *his* question. "When we get outta here, call the cops. The stiff out there tried to rob the place and some Robin Hood you never saw before showed up, saved the day, and then took off. Sound okay to you?"

Buster nodded in agreement. "As if I had made it up myself."

"Everybody's carryin' these days," Rico said. "So, they oughta swallow it."

The body wasn't visible to anyone entering the café unless they walked all the way up to the counter, but Buster went back to make sure no customers wandered in and got close enough to discover it.

Rico turned back to Jean, who was swiftly repairing the damage the gag had caused to her makeup. "Nose powdered?"

Jean finished dabbing a hint of powder on her nose and chin and freshened her lipstick. She tucked her purse under her arm and nodded, a little self-consciously.

"Then let's go," Rico said.

Rico and Jean returned to the front of the store where Buster stood behind the counter, a little uneasily. He walked around to escort them to the door. He and Rico shook hands and Jean gave him a big hug and thanked him again. "We'll be outta your hair in a sec'," Rico said. Then he and Jean went outside to wait for Paul and Evelyn.

Paul's car showed up in about two minutes. Rico opened the rear door and he and Jean got in. Paul turned around and said, "Hello, Jean. Are you all right?"

Jean smiled. "I'm fine. Thanks."

Evelyn turned around.

"Jean, this is Evelyn," Rico introduced her.

"Hi," Evelyn said warmly, as though she was happy to meet her.

"Evelyn, this is Jean," Rico said.

"Hello," Jean said shyly.

Rico glanced back at the store and saw Buster peering out, obviously waiting for them to leave so he could call the police and rid himself of the body behind his counter.

"Now that we all know each other, how about a bite to eat?" Rico said. "I'm starving."

"You don't like Buster's?" Paul said.

"He's closing."

"So, what happened back there?" Paul asked.

"Nothing," Rico said. "The guy had followed her like I suspected. I gave him a piece of my mind."

"And?"

"He didn't say a word."

Paul, who had been facing forward, turned and cast a dubious glance in Rico's direction. The expression on Rico's face was as impassive as ever. Paul smiled to himself, turned around and started driving. "I know a place," he said.

They stopped at a mom and pop soul food restaurant in the heart of the South Side, where the house specialties were barbequed ribs, fried chicken, fried catfish, collard greens, macaroni and cheese, and candied yams. When Paul pulled into the parking lot in front of the store, he asked Rico. "This suit your taste?"

"How did you know?" Rico said. "When was the last time we were here, Jean?"

"I don't know, maybe a month ago."

"I like a thick steak and a salad as much as the next guy, but this is comfort food," Rico said. "We probably eat this kind of food more often than you do, counselor," Rico said.

"Not more often than I do," Evelyn said.

"Well, I guess the joke's on me," Paul said sheepishly.

They went inside and sat in one of the four red vinyl-covered booths. Paul ordered ribs, Rico ordered fried chicken, and Evelyn and Jean ordered catfish. Once the food arrived, the conversation turned, awkwardly at first, to the rift between Paul and Evelyn caused by Rico.

"You obviously convinced her, counselor," Rico said. "How did you answer her very legitimate complaints?"

"I told her that I don't agree with your lifestyle, but I owed you this much."

"I'm flattered, counselor, but I don't like people owing me anything."

"That's not exactly a secret," Paul said, a little peeved. "So, let's just call it even."

"You do what you want," Rico said, neither angered nor pleased by Paul's remark. "I'll do what I want."

Chastened, Paul said nothing, but Evelyn seized the initiative to unburden herself to Rico. She first turned to Paul. "What frightens me is that... Paul, we talked about this..." Then she turned to Rico and said plainly, "What frightens me is deep down inside I think he admires you and wants to emulate you."

Rico leaned back in his chair and folded his arms across his chest. "Wow," he said. "Emulate is a big word – but I guess not for a professor." She smiled a little, involuntarily, at his dry humor. Rico noticed but said nothing. Instead, he cast his gaze in Paul's direction. "Counselor, you and I are alike in some small ways. I like words and I like jazz, for instance, and tonight I found out we both like the same kind of food. I think we both keep our word and we both pay our debts. But I'm sure none of those similarities are what make Evelyn here a little nervous." He turned to her and this time a hint of a smile played at the corners of his mouth. "Evelyn, all I can say is I am what I am. I make no excuses. But that's me, not him."

Evelyn persisted. "Look at your matching shoulder holsters," she said. "Is powder-blue that popular a color? And those sunglasses of yours. Paul has a pair that are almost identical."

Embarrassed, Paul rolled his eyes and slowly shook his head from side to side.

"Mere coincidence," Rico said. "Blue is my favorite color. Maybe it's his, too. And as for the sunglasses, obviously, we both have excellent taste. Look, maybe a long time ago I coulda been like him, but not now, no matter how many two-dollar words I throw around. Same with him. He couldn't be like me if his life depended on it."

"You may be sure, but sometimes I'm not," Evelyn said.

Rico placed both hands on the table and leaned forward. "Want another reason?" he said. "Jean, you mentioned how I never talk about my ol' man, and you, counselor, you wanted to know what happened to him." He paused and gazed into Jean's eyes. "I put a bullet in his brain when I was sixteen, and I'd do it again today," he said calmly, without emotion.

Paul and Evelyn regarded each other, the same look of shock on each of their faces. Jean gasped audibly and brought a hand to her mouth. "Rico, no!"

"After you waste your own father, it's not hard anymore," he said. And then, while everyone searched for the right words to say in response, Rico said, "Now, anyone for dessert?"

There was a long, stunned silence. Jean buried her face in her hands.

"I guess not," Rico said.

Paul cleared his throat and said, "Maybe it's not my place to ask, but..."

140

"Why?" Rico said, finishing his sentence. "Because he begged me to. He had cancer and it was rippin' him apart, but he couldn't do it himself. So, I did. He held the gun and I pulled the trigger."

"And everyone thought he committed suicide," Paul said.

"Very perspicacious, counselor."

"You should have told me," Jean said earnestly, her eyes welling.

"I would have eventually. Now seemed like as good a time as any." Then he turned to Evelyn, one eyebrow raised. "Got me figured out yet?"

Evelyn lowered her head and looked down and stared at nothing in particular, searching for the right words. A moment later she raised her head and looked squarely at Rico. "I guess it helps explain some things," she said. "The effect something like that would have had on the mind of a sixteen-year-old... to have to do something like that... well, I can't imagine."

"Please, no psychoanalysis," Rico said. "What I do is what I do. I'm good at it. I like it and I got scruples – not your kind maybe – but my own, which suits me fine."

"If I were to suggest that you let the police take over from this point on," Evelyn said, "I suppose that would be naïve of me."

"Quite." Rico said.

"So, what are we going to do now?" Paul asked.

"Have dessert," Rico said. "We missed out on having pie at Buster's."

Chapter Twenty-Two

After Gus reached the corner of Cleveland's street and turned at the intersection, he said to Larry, "I'll drop you at your place and head back home."

"Then what?

"Then nothing."

"What about the woman?" Larry asked.

"You recognize her?"

"Never seen her before."

"Then, nothing, like I said before."

"She probably couldn't see you on the other side of the car, but what if she got a good look at me?" Larry asked.

"She didn't."

"How do you know?"

"I know," Gus said.

Larry hesitated to challenge Gus, especially after the scene at Gus's house earlier that day, but this was important. He took a deep breath and let his words spill out slowly. "Well, would you mind tellin' me *how* you know?"

"Simple," Gus said. "When did you first see her?"

"When she screamed."

"Okay, you shot Cleveland and then she screamed, right?"

"Yeah."

"What did she do right after that?"

Cleveland closed his eyes and thought for a couple of seconds. "I don't know."

"'Cause after that last shot, I hit the gas and tore outta there, right?" Larry nodded.

"And that was about the same time she screamed, right?"

"Yeah, I guess so," Larry said.

"Was she still in the window when I hit the gas?"

"I don't know."

"'Cause you didn't keep lookin' at her after she screamed, did you?" Gus said.

"I guess I was lookin' straight ahead by then."

"And if she was lookin' at you, all she could see was the side of your face or maybe even the back of your head, right?"

"I guess."

"On top of all that," Gus said, "It's startin' to get dark, ain't it?"

"Yeah."

"And she was, what, thirty or forty yards away?"

"Somethin' like that."

Gus paused a moment to let his analysis sink in. "See what I'm gettin' at?"

"Yeah, I see, but I'm still not sure."

"Kid, didn't anybody ever tell you that nothin' is ever certain in this life except death and taxes?"

Larry said nothing, just sank into his seat belligerently and folded his arms across his chest.

"Okay, let me tell you a story," Gus said. "My lawyer Jimmie Fox always says if the only thing they got on you is eye-witness testimony, you got a good shot at beatin' the rap. Fingerprints or DNA, not so much. Know why? Eye-witness testimony is, what did he say? "Notoriously unreliable." That's it. Notoriously unreliable. Here is the proof."

"Jimmie told me the first day of law school, his professor is teachin' criminal law and he's standin' in front of the class in a big room, and a few minutes after he starts talkin' two guys rush in from a side door and start beatin' the crap outta him. Then they lift his wallet and hustle out the side door. This only takes a few seconds and the whole class is sittin' there in shock with their mouths wide open. By the time anybody gets up enough nerve to try to help the professor, the guys who worked him over are out the door."

"Now here is the kicker. The whole damn thing was staged. The professor faked everything. He asked the two guys to wait outside and then he asked the class to describe 'em. It was a big room, but a lot of people were sittin' right up front, close to where this happened. Now here is the real kicker. Everybody had a different description. Height, body build, hair color, everything. One guy was black, and one was white and some of 'em didn't even get that right!"

"Feel better now?" Gus said.

"It's a funny story."

"It *is* a funny story, but even if everything I said turns out to be bullshit and she picks you out of a line up, we got one more ace in the hole. When 'whoever it was' that whacked Cleveland did it, you and me was havin' dinner at my house with my wife and two or three other guys I'll call when I get home."

That seemed to satisfy Larry, and he was quiet for the rest of the ride to his apartment, where Gus dropped him off with instructions to stay put for the rest of the night. Gus ditched the stolen car a few blocks away from his house and walked home from there. When he got there, his wife was waiting up for him. She was pacing the floor when she heard him turn the key in the lock on the front door and hurried to meet him. When he opened the door, she rushed into his arms and held him so tight he could hardly breathe. She didn't let go until he spoke.

"Hey, hey, what's this all about?" he said, surprised by the intensity of her embrace.

"I told you I'd wait up."

"I know but I told you there was nothin' to worry about, right?"

"I know but I just ... " She paused and lowered her eyes, wondering whether she should continue.

He took a step back, raised her chin with the back of his hand, and looked into her eyes. "Just what?"

"I just had a feeling – a bad feeling that something might happen to you."

He kissed her forehead. "What did I tell you? It was just a piece of business. Besides, I'm gettin' too old for that rough stuff."

It was unlike her to be so worried about him. She didn't nag him about his affairs, and she almost always took whatever he did, or whatever happened to him, in stride and he appreciated that. He didn't want to upset her anymore that evening, so since he still didn't think an alibi would be necessary, he figured he would wait until later to decide whether he needed to raise the subject with her at all.

She smiled, put her arm around his waist, and walked with him into the living room, where they plopped down on the sofa in front of the TV, held hands, and searched for something to watch.

Gus had never said directly to Larry and Cleveland, "Do not whack Koblentz!" or specific words to that effect. But mob bosses seldom are so direct, and their underlings know it. In fact, because they can never be sure who is listening or who might be wearing a wire, often they are intentionally indirect. For example, instead of saying, "Don't whack Joe Blow," one of them might say, "Some people might not like it if somethin' happened to Joe," or, "It might not be too good if somethin' happened to Joe."

So, there could be no misunderstanding when Gus had said, "I don't want a war over this," or when he'd said, "Think about it and when you make up your mind, come back and see me. We'll talk about it, okay?" He had meant he didn't want *anyone* else killed over this, not just Rico. Nevertheless, despite his warning, to use his metaphor, Cleveland had waltzed into his neighborhood, marched right up to his front door, strolled inside, and taken a crap on Gus's living room floor – a mess Gus had had to clean it up.

Cleveland's defiance had been a slap in the face, which is why Gus had gotten personally involved, something he hadn't done in years.

But there was something else. He'd sensed that his underlings might be getting restless and starting to feel that his control over the neighborhood was slipping. He'd let Larry get away with far too much. Obviously, in his mind, that was because Larry was "blood." But others noticed things and Gus thought they might start wondering how much was really blood and how much was because he was starting to lose his grip on the neighborhood. Nobody said anything out loud, of course, but no one had to. When you'd been in charge as long as Gus had, you could sense it. Ordering Larry to whack Cleveland was his way of sending a message to the doubters. Driving the getaway car himself put an exclamation point on it.

Larry was worried. He had been pacing the living room floor at his apartment since Gus dropped him off. The swiftness with which Gus had made the decision to take Cleveland out had caught him off guard. He had already gunned Cleveland down before he realized he hadn't yet broken the news to Gus that he'd kidnapped Jean to get to Rico. He prayed that everything had gone okay with that scheme because, whether it had or not, he knew now that he was going to have to have a much more difficult conversation with Gus than he'd originally anticipated. If the scheme had gone awry, though, that conversation was going to be infinitely more difficult, plus, with Cleveland now gone, there was nobody else he could blame.

Larry punched in a number on his cell. When the person on the other end answered, he asked hopefully, "Any word?"

"Yeah, it's not good."

Larry sighed. "Lemme have it."

"The girl showed up outside the old guy's apartment. She got away from Weasel, but he caught up with her at Buster's. Rico showed up there, capped Weasel and left with the girl."

"Shit, shit, shit," Larry mumbled. "Where the hell were you?"

"Outside Rico' place, watchin' it, like you told me."

Larry thought for a moment. "They won't be stupid enough to go there or to her place tonight. I'm at my apartment. You and Dennis meet me here as soon as you can round him up."

Gus had to make a call, too. After ten minutes, his wife had fallen asleep with her head on his shoulder. He cautiously eased away while gently lowering her head on to a throw pillow on the sofa. Then, being careful not to awaken her, he slowly raised her legs onto the sofa.

He called Rico while standing in the doorway between the living room and the kitchen so that he could keep an eye on his wife. When Rico saw Gus's number on the caller I.D., he said, "Excuse me, I gotta take this." Paul was curious but said nothing, and neither did Jean or Evelyn. Rico got up and strolled to the men's room. It was unoccupied but he checked inside each stall to make sure.

"I was expectin' you to call me first," Gus said.

"I bet."

"Where are you?"

"Here and there."

"I guess you heard," Gus said.

"About?"

"Koblentz."

"Yeah, I did," Rico said.

Gus peered into the living room to make sure his wife was still asleep. "Rico, it was Cleveland."

"I thought you had him under control."

"The guy just went berserk. But don't worry. He's under control now."

"How so?'

"We nailed him outside his place."

Paul came in and, arms folded, leaned against the wall a few feet from Rico so that he was close enough to hear him. Rico looked up, recognized Paul, and continued talking. "Gus, it wasn't Cleveland."

"What?"

"It was Larry."

"Bullshit!"

"You know a character named Weasel?"

"Yeah, he works for me."

"He know Larry?"

"Sure, but –"

Rico glanced at Paul and made eye contact. "I just put a bullet through his forehead," Rico said. "He was lyin' in wait for Jean at Koblentz's place. He probably thought Larry was takin' orders from you."

Shocked, Gus didn't immediately answer. While Rico waited, he checked for a reaction from Paul, who made a point of showing no emotion at all.

"I just talked to Larry and a friend of Cleveland's. Cleveland admitted killin' the old guy."

"The friend lied," Rico said bluntly.

Gus hesitated before answering. "I believe him," he said but he no longer did.

"You believe what you want."

"Jesus, Jesus," Gus said at last. "Lemme talk to Larry."

"You already talked to him and look where it got you," Rico said firmly.

"I hafta try."

"No matter what he says, I can't trust him. *No deference and no respect*. Either you do it or I will."

"Rico, he's my nephew," Gus pleaded.

"And this is my neck."

"You puttin' me in a tough spot."

"It's the same spot I'm in," Rico pointed out.

Gus pondered his choices. It only took him a couple of seconds. "You win," he said. "But you do it. I can't."

Gus hung up and Rico disconnected. He glanced at Paul again, curious to see his reaction. Again, however, there was none.

Chapter Twenty-Three

Evelyn hadn't objected when Paul excused himself to join Rico. Although she had privately decided when she and Paul made up to give him free rein in matters concerning Rico, it was still difficult, so she gave herself a pat on the back. She was still silently congratulating herself when Jean asked her a question.

"So, how long have you two been together?"

"Just a few years," Evelyn said. "How about you?"

"Longer. How did you meet?"

"We've actually known each other since college, but we weren't together then. We might have been, but I was pretty serious about someone else, actually the man I married. I bumped into Paul in Honolulu a couple of years ago at a souvenir shop. We were both looking for post cards. It was the strangest thing. I was behind the card holder, spinning it in one direction and he was in front of it spinning it in the other direction. When we saw each other, we were both in shock. Paul told me his wife had been killed by a drunk driver while they were jogging a year earlier, and he was just getting over it. And I had just decided to divorce my cheating husband, so we had a lot of catching up to do.... I suppose you know the rest."

Jean nodded. "Most of it anyway."

"I know you care for him and all... But I just have to ask, how do you handle it?"

"I tell myself nobody ever died because of him that didn't deserve it. If somebody dies who didn't deserve it, I don't wanna hear about it."

"Paul and I almost did."

"I know," Jean acknowledged. "But you didn't."

"Two other people did."

"Good people?"

Evelyn hesitated. They hadn't been so good. "They didn't deserve to die."

"If Rico did it, he thought so."

Evelyn wanted to say, '*But he's not God! What gave him the right?*' Instead she asked, "What if he was wrong?"

Jean paused, struggling to convince herself as much as Evelyn. "It's his call, not mine. He's the one who has to live with it."

"You're a better woman than I am," Evelyn said, shaking her head.

Jean shook her head. "It's not easy. It's hard. But it gets easier. Everything except worrying about him. That's the one thing that doesn't get any easier."

"You know, Paul and I almost broke up... well, there was something else, but mostly because of – because of all this."

"You mean because he helped Rico?" Jean asked.

"Yes. I'm resigned to Paul's decision. That's why I came back, plus I don't want to lose him. But that doesn't mean I have to agree with it."

"Maybe you don't but I think you should try to understand, for his sake – Paul's I mean. He's a standup guy. Rico's right. He *is* like him in some ways."

Evelyn sighed. "I know... only too well... But you never told me how you met Rico."

"I was at a bar with some girlfriends, and Rico was there with Jerry, a friend of his, a real nice guy. I liked him a lot. He died – no, he was killed - a while back."

"I'm sorry," Evelyn said.

"You don't have to be," Jean said. "I was pretty upset about it but, like Rico said, it was the life he chose – same as Rico.... Anyway, Jerry came over to our table and struck up a conversation with me, and Rico just hung back until one of my girlfriends came over to his table and started talking to him. He ignored her, in a nice way, I mean, and I wasn't feelin' it with Jerry. There was just somethin' between Rico and me, and Jerry and my girlfriend saw it, so we just switched partners. And we've been together ever since."

The two women had vastly different backgrounds, not unlike Rico and Paul in some ways. Evelyn came from privileged circumstances. Her parents were successful architects and she was a pampered only child. They debated whether to send her to private schools but philosophically they preferred public schools as one way of grounding her and, to the extent possible, preventing her from acquiring an attitude of entitlement. Thus, the main reason they chose their upscale suburb was the superb reputation of its public schools. They could afford to have a maid but chose not to and insisted from an early age that Evelyn do chores around the house. From the age of sixteen through college, she always had a part-time job.

By contrast, Jean's background was anything but privileged. She had three younger sisters and her parents both worked in retail sales before her father died in a one-car traffic accident when Jean was thirteen. Unfortunately, he had no life insurance. Although she was a good student and wanted to go to college, when she graduated from high school, she took a job as a waitress to help her mother out with bills.

Despite their different backgrounds, what Evelyn and Jean had in common was that both were empathetic, caring people who were concerned for the safety of the people in their lives. That was enough for them to have made a connection.

There was a lull in the conversation between the two women when, to fill the gap, Evelyn asked, "Do you have family in town?"

"My mother and three younger sisters."

"It's just my mother and father and me," Evelyn said. "I think they spoiled me."

"You don't act spoiled. If you were a man, I'd say you seem like a pretty regular guy."

"I know some people who might disagree, but thanks for the compliment." Evelyn smiled.

There was another momentary lull and Jean said, "You know, you asking about my family got me thinking about them. I haven't talked to my mother in quite a while. My sisters either. Sometimes I miss them."

"That's too bad," Evelyn said, wanting to ask why but thinking it was too personal and restraining herself.

But Jean explained, surprising herself with her candor. "She objects to the way I earn my living, but I guess any mother would."

"But I'll bet she and your sisters still love you."

"It doesn't matter at this point."

"But you said you miss them sometimes."

"I guess I did. I do, but I don't need them anymore. I can take care of myself."

"Like Rico?"

"Yeah, like him."

"Listen," Evelyn said. "I barely know you so I hope you don't take this the wrong way, but it sounds like you're trying to convince yourself of something you may not really believe."

Jean laughed out loud.

"What did I say?" Evelyn asked.

"I was just thinking. What you said, it may be very perspicacious of you."

Evelyn laughed and Jean joined in. After a moment both women fell silent again. Evelyn reached over and placed her hand on Jean's. "Why don't you call her?"

Jean sighed heavily, letting her breath escape slowly. "Maybe I will."

"There's no time like the present," Evelyn said. "Not very original, but true."

Jean took her cell out of her purse and set it on the table.

"I'll give you some privacy," Evelyn said, standing.

"You don't have to," Jean said tentatively. She wasn't sure she wanted to be alone when she talked to her mother.

"No, you go ahead. I'll go and powder my nose."

Evelyn left and Jean stared at the phone for a long moment. Finally, she took a deep breath and punched in her mother 's number. *'Maybe she's not there.'* The phone rang once, twice, three times. *'I hope she's not there.'* She started to put the phone down when her mother answered.

"Ma, is that you?"

"Yes, it's me," her mother said, her voice gruff and impatient. "What do you want?"

Jean hesitated. With only two short sentences her mother had confirmed her fears. No matter, she was determined not to let her disappointment show. "I just called to say hello. It's been a while."

"Not long enough."

"Ma, how can you be so cruel?"

"I'm just bein' honest."

"But I'm still your daughter."

"Neither one of us can change that." Her mother retorted sharply.

"I guess this will be a short conversation, then." Jean said. "I just thought –"

"Jean, you chose the kind of life you're livin' all by yourself; you're a common whore and I just can't abide it."

"I'm not a thief. I'm not an addict. And I'm not hurting anybody." Jean protested.

"Except yourself – and your family."

Jean bit her tongue. *'At least I tried.'* She wiped away a single tear. "How are Peggy, and Janet, and Mary Alice?"

"All fine."

"Well, are they in school, working, still living at home ...? Tell me *something.*"

"They all live here with me, same as always."

"Is that all you intend to tell me?"

"Jean, they're all nice, respectable young ladies. And I wanna keep 'em that way. Now, you can call this number anytime and talk to 'em. I can't stop you. But I wish you wouldn't. They know about the kinda life you're livin' and they know it's wrong. I thought about tellin' 'em you was dead but I didn't. I told 'em I didn't know where you was, which is true. I wish you would just stay outta their lives."

Jean shook her head. "You can hate me all you want, but I'm sorry you had to turn them against me."

"I don't hate you. I hate what you did to yourself. And like I said, I just told your sisters the truth."

Jean had heard about as much from her mother as she could take. Talking any longer would just make things worse. "Ma, I'm glad you don't hate me because I don't hate you. If you ever want to talk to me, you can reach me at this number. I'll listen to whatever you have to say. But you can't ask me to never talk to my sisters again. The next time I call your number, it'll be to talk to them."

She disconnected.

Evelyn had stood at a polite distance outside the ladies' room while Jean talked on the phone, and from her vantage point, she could see Jean as she talked on her cell. After Jean disconnected and put the phone on the table, she waited thirty seconds and then started back. She reached the table just as Jean wiped another tear from her eye.

"Is everything okay?" Evelyn asked, sitting.

"Everything's great," Jean said sarcastically.

"I'm sorry," Evelyn said, crestfallen. "I shouldn't have pushed you into calling."

"No, it's not your fault. I needed to confirm what I think I already knew, and now was as good a time as any."

"Is there anything I can do?"

"No, but thanks for asking. I can't do anything about the way my mother feels, but maybe it's not too late to reach my sisters. I'm damn well gonna try."

"Good," Evelyn said.

During Rico's phone conversation with Gus, Paul had heard him mention Larry's name, and when the conversation ended, Paul asked, "Is this guy Larry behind all this?"

Curt as always, Rico answered, "Yeah."

"And you intend to go after him."

"I do."

Paul let Rico's answer hang in the air for a second then returned to the subject they were discussing before Rico's phone rang. "You know, what you said out there about me – it didn't change Evelyn's mind."

"I said my piece for her sake, but she's right, up to a point. And you know it."

Their eyes met and, stone-faced and silent, each held the other's gaze. After a few seconds, Paul said, "If you're done here, we might as well go back outside."

By the time they reached their table, Jean had composed herself and was telling Evelyn stories about happier times in her family before her father's fatal car crash. She was just holding it together, but when she saw Rico, the dam burst, and she started to cry.

"What brought that on?" Rico asked.

"Nothing," Jean said. "Just girl talk. It's been a tough day."

"Girl talk?" Rico said. "I'd hate to see you when you're talkin' about somethin' serious."

Jean wiped away her tears and smiled brightly, but Rico knew there was something more. "You wanna talk in private?" he asked.

"Please," Paul said, standing. "Evelyn and I can step outside."

"No, please sit," Jean said. To Rico she added, "I talked to my mother is all."

"Oh," Rico said, needing no further explanation for her state of mind.

"We can talk about it later," Jean said. "I mean, if you want to."

He didn't want to. To him Jean's mother was a lost cause and Jean shouldn't be wasting her time trying to talk to her. His attitude was, why should Jean waste her breath if her mother couldn't see in her own beautiful, kind daughter what Rico saw as plain as day? *'To hell with her and good riddance.'*

But he didn't say any of that. Instead, he said, gruffly, "If you want to, then I want to." For once he had dissembled. And he didn't know why.

Taken aback, Jean furrowed her brow. Then she smiled. "If that's the way you feel, then the phone call wasn't that bad after all."

Rico smiled back. He still didn't know why he'd lied to Jean. And it bothered him.

They finished eating in relative silence. Neither Evelyn nor Jean asked who had called Rico or what was discussed. Obviously, neither man wanted to discuss it. Evelyn resolved to bite her tongue and ask Paul later. Jean wasn't sure she'd ever find out, but she knew Rico would tell her when he was ready.

Outside the restaurant Rico, leaning on his cane, turned to Paul. "Do me a favor. Drop Jean off at a hotel. They may still be watchin' her place."

Before Paul could answer, Evelyn said, "She can stay with us."

Mildly surprised, Paul chimed in, "Sure."

"I don't want to be a bother," Jean said.

"You won't be," Evelyn said.

"Won't they be watching your place, too?" Paul asked Rico.

"They might, but I'm not goin' there – at least not yet."

"Then where?" Paul asked.

"Where Jean left the car. They should be watchin' it, too. But I'd rather get that shot to hell than my place."

"I'll grab a cab for the ladies. Then I'll take you," Paul said.

"You can drop me a block or so away. I don't want you to get too close. You might cramp my style," Rico said.

"Just come back in one piece," Jean said.

"Paul, you'll come right back?" Evelyn pressed.

"He will, or he'll have me to deal with," Rico said.

"What a motley crew we make," Evelyn said, not quite believing herself.

"I prefer 'multifarious'," Rico said. "Jean?"

"Multifarious," Jean repeated, pronouncing each syllable distinctly.

Everybody smiled, even Rico.

Paul hailed a cab and waited for it to drive off with Jean and Evelyn before he started his own car. As they approached his car, Rico raised a hand, signaling Paul to stop. "This is as far as you go, counselor."

"You have it all figured out."

"Yeah, pretty much. One guy should be watchin' the car. When he sees me, he'll follow me and call for reinforcements."

"What if he tries something right there?"

"He'll want some help. They already lost one guy tonight."

"But suppose he's not alone?" Paul asked.

"Then that might even the odds."

'*Not cocky, just damned confident,*' Paul said to himself.

Rico collected his cane, opened the car door and got out. "Later, counselor."

He rounded a corner and slowly made his way down a dimly lit, deserted street. He didn't turn around to look behind him, but his eyes darted from side to side in search of signs of trouble. Finally, he reached the car, unlocked the door, and stood motionless. There was only silence. After a moment, he suddenly spun around, balancing himself on his cane. A look of alarm washed over his face. He opened the car door, jumped inside, and started it. Burning rubber, he retraced his route until he reached the place where Paul had dropped him off. He slammed on the brakes. Paul was still there.

"What happened?" Paul asked, alarmed.

"Get in."

Paul hastily got out of his car, locked it, and slid into the passenger seat next to Rico. "What is it?"

"Which way to your place?" Rico asked calmly but firmly.

"No!" Paul shouted as Rico sped away.

Chapter Twenty-Four

As Paul and Rico raced toward Paul's condo, Paul reached for his cell phone. "I'm calling the police."

"What are you gonna tell them?" Rico asked. "You have a hunch somebody may get killed? Good luck."

Paul put his cell away.

Several blocks away, the taxi carrying Evelyn and Jean pulled up outside Paul and Evelyn's condo. In a solitary parked car across the street, Larry, behind the wheel, and three other men, faces in the shadows, sat silently waiting.

The two women got out and the taxi drove away. At that point, the man in the front passenger seat of the car across the street said tersely, "Get 'em."

The two men in the back seat got out and started crossing the street in the direction of the condo as Evelyn and Jean neared the entrance to the building. Save for an occasional random vehicle driving by, the street was deadly silent. Almost simultaneously, the two women heard the footsteps approaching behind them, and almost in unison they turned around and stopped. They saw the two men, both taller and bigger than average, who had already crossed from the other side of the street and who were now stepping onto the tree lawn in front of them. Still several yards away from the women, the men said nothing but kept moving, quickening their pace as they got ever closer.

The street was well lit, and the women could now see the men's faces, ominous and determined, as they steadily closed the distance between them. Jean glanced at Evelyn, her eyes asking; *'Do you know them?'* Evelyn understood and shook her head. Burly and grim-faced, the thugs clearly were neither a couple of neighbors Evelyn had never met, nor a pair of lost strangers looking for directions.

Evelyn turned her head and eyed her front door. She was too far away. She hadn't even started searching for her key yet amid the clutter inside her purse. Locating it would consume precious seconds. She calculated that if she made a dash for the door, she wouldn't even have time to find the key and get it into the lock before the men managed to overtake her. With Paul's help, she had managed to elude a deadly pursuer in Honolulu and later had confronted a hostile loan shark in his office in Chicago. Both crises had made her a stronger woman, but Paul was by her side on both occasions, lending moral, and once physical, support. This time she and Jean were alone. Needing encouragement, she glanced at Jean.

When Evelyn's eyes found Jean's, they were cold and resolute. They said she would stand her ground. A rape survivor and a kidnap victim only hours earlier, she did not intend to be a victim again. She looked around for anything she could use as a weapon and saw nothing within reach. All she could do now was hope against hope that the men were not armed and stand shoulder to shoulder with Evelyn, bracing for a fight she feared they would not win.

Jean stared hard into the men's eyes, and for the first time their grim masks fell away. They both grinned, the leer of a bully relishing an impending confrontation with someone weaker than themselves.

At that moment, Rico's car, burning rubber, rounded a corner onto Paul and Evelyn's street some fifty yards away from their condo. The back end of the lone car parked across the street loomed in front of Rico and Paul. Their car fast approaching, they could make out, in the glare of their headlights, two men seated in the front seat of the parked car. Rico hit his bright high-beam lights. Shading their eyes, the two men turned around. Larry was behind the wheel.

The other was Gus in the passenger seat.

As their car drew closer to the parked car, Paul saw Evelyn and Jean in his front yard standing feet apart from the two men, who now turned their backs to the women and fixed their gaze on Rico's speeding car. He rolled down his window and yelled, "Get down, get down!" The two women dropped to the ground. The two men unholstered their 45's and, training them on Rico's car barreling down the street, they fired several shots at it.

"Get down!" Rico yelled to Paul and lowered his body as much as possible while Paul did the same.

A few rounds penetrated the side of the car, buried themselves in the front and rear seat cushions, and went no further. A few passed through one side panel and came to rest in the other, and a few passed all the way through the rear windows on both sides of the car. One round passed directly in front of Paul then Rico, and mercifully grazed only the top of the dashboard before exiting the open window on the other side.

But Rico's car, now zigzagging from side to side, kept coming.

Hearing the shots, seeing the full glare from Rico's headlights coming ever closer, but unable to see inside his car, Larry and Gus at first continued to shield their eyes from the blinding headlights until they realized that Rico's car was roaring toward them. Guessing Rico's intentions but not entirely sure, Paul looked up at him. "What are you going to do?" he asked, his pulse quickening and his voice rising slightly.

"Hold on, counselor."

Panicked, Larry and Gus reached for their door handles but before either could get his door open, Rico's car slammed into the rear of theirs, causing air bags to deploy in both cars. Guns blazing, the two hoodlums across the street abandoned the women and started sprinting back across the street. Rico and Paul freed themselves from the tangle of air bags. Rico unholstered his weapon.

"Get out on this side," Rico said and tumbled out.

Paul started to follow, fighting his way through the jumble of air bags, when he saw the men approaching. They were within feet of the car. Joining Rico without being seen was now impossible. He unholstered his .45 and sank down in his seat as far as he could. He would have to show himself to get a shot at either of them. He took a deep breath. *'This could be it.'* He slowly raised his head until he was eye level with the bottom of the open window. He looked out. They were gone. They hadn't seen him. They'd assumed he'd gotten out on the other side.

The men had arrived just as Rico rolled out of the car. One of them had hastily checked the passenger side and, in fact, had missed Paul because of the airbags blocking the view. Not seeing him, they'd gone straight for the other side. One man had approached from the front of the car and the other from the back. When they'd reached the car, each man had kneeled down beside it, using it for cover, intending to emerge simultaneously and catch Rico and Paul in a crossfire. Unable to see each other, however, their timing had been off by a hair, which meant that for a split-second Rico would only have one target to worry about.

Grasping his Sig Sauer with both hands, the barrel pointed skyward, Rico sat on the ground, his elbows pressed against his torso, his back braced against the side of the car, and waited, watching the mirror.

Not seeing the two men, Paul tried to open his door. It was stuck.

The man behind the car approached Rico first. As soon as he appeared in the sideview mirror, Rico pivoted to his left, extended and locked his arms, and fired a single bullet which pierced the man's heart. The dying gunman got off one wild shot as he was falling to the ground. By then, Rico had already pivoted back to his right and was ready when an instant later the second gunman emerged from in front of the car, only to suffer the same fate as the first shooter. After he showed himself, he had to sight Rico and take aim. Rico didn't need to do either. Arms still outstretched and locked, he shot the man as soon as he appeared – once in the forehead and once in the heart for good measure. Unlike the first shooter, this one didn't even get a shot off.

Paul heard the three shots. He gambled that Rico had killed the two gunmen. He took another deep breath. "Rico," he whispered.

"I'm fine," Rico whispered back. "Be careful. The other two guys are still in the car. Get out on your side and wait."

"The door is stuck but I'll try again."

He pushed hard and the door gave a little. He pushed harder, putting his shoulder into it, and the door slowly creaked open. He scrambled out. He lay on his stomach with his .45 pointed at Larry and Gus's car. And he waited.

Because their engine was idling, the airbags in Gus and Larry's car also deployed, but both men had unfastened their seatbelts as they sat waiting. That was a recipe for potentially serious injuries or even death, when the airbags deployed with nothing to hold the two men in place. They had been lucky. They were shaken up and disoriented but otherwise no worse for wear. They were, however, even slower than Paul had been to get out of their car.

Hearing the shots emanating from the driver's side of Rico's car, Gus struggled out first, signaling to Larry to stay put. Unsure of the fate of his two gunmen, holding his .45, he carefully dropped to his hands and knees. He didn't see Paul lying down, .45 in hand, resting on his elbows on the ground behind him. Like the two dead shooters, Gus had assumed that Paul must have gotten out on the driver's side of the car. He calculated that anyone or no one might have survived the gun battle he'd heard from inside the car, but his money was on Rico. Grasping his .45 in both hands, he stretched his arms across the hood of the car and waited for Rico to stand.

After waiting for only a few seconds, suddenly what had been an afterthought in his whirling mind now seized Gus's brain and held it tightly. For the first time he wondered whether Rico's front seat passenger might still be in the car or, worse, whether he had already gotten out on the passenger side. Without moving his arms, he turned his head ever so slightly and out of the corner of his eye he glimpsed Paul – and his .45 pointed at straight him.

Paul said nothing but stared Gus in the eye. He was prepared to defend himself, but he hadn't decided whether to fire the first shot. He held his breath.

The wheels in Gus's brain started to turn. '*Should I try to talk my way out of this? And if I do, when Rico hears my voice, is he gonna simply stand up and blow my head off? The guy on the ground hasn't pulled the trigger yet, so maybe he won't. But if Rico's alive, he damn sure will, as soon as I open my mouth.*' Abruptly, his mind made up, Gus swung his arms and the .45 around to his left, but before he could point the weapon downward toward Paul, Paul fired three times. Gus dropped his gun and his body began its slow descent to the pavement. When the shots rang out, Rico had stood instantly, pointing his .45 at the space Gus no longer occupied. He had risen just in time to hear Gus's body brush against the car as it collapsed on to the ground.

"Counselor, you hit?" Rico yelled.

"No, I'm fine," Paul responded, still stretched out on the ground on the other side of the car.

That momentary distraction gave Larry, gun in his hand, the opportunity to tumble out and scramble to the front of the car and then crouch down beside it just as a city bus lumbered slowly down the street toward him. As the bus approached his hiding place, he darted in front of it an instant before Rico noticed him. The bus screeched to a halt and as Rico took aim, Larry ran around it, using it as a shield. Paul, who had rapidly gotten to his feet, noticed Larry the same time Rico did. He holstered his .45 and they both gave chase. Rico, slowed by his injured leg, stopped after a few yards and again took aim at Larry, but he was out of range. Paul sprinted ahead.

Larry didn't look back. His focus was now on catching up to Evelyn and Jean and using them as a bargaining chip. As he got closer, the two women could see Paul racing toward them and gaining on Larry. Their instinct was to try to reach the building door but, having dropped to the ground earlier and not moved since, they were no closer to the door now than they had been when Rico rammed Gus and Larry's car.

And there was an added wrinkle. Similar thoughts crossed the minds of both women. The other two men, they reasoned, while certainly menacing, had not brandished any weapons until they fired at Rico's car. But Larry was plainly carrying a gun as he bolted toward them. '*Would he shoot at them if they ran? Could Paul catch up with Larry in time if they just stood still? Would anything they did cause Larry to turn around and see Paul, and maybe kill him?*'

The women froze.

Paul, who had run track in college, rapidly gained ground on Larry. Although the night was quiet, the sound of Larry's own footsteps and heavy breathing masked the sound of Paul's feet as he sprinted after him. Only when Paul was barely a few yards behind him did Larry think he heard someone following him. He slowed and started to turn his head.

Evelyn noticed and tried to distract him. "What do you want?" she yelled loudly.

"Yeah, what is it?" Jean chimed in.

Larry glanced back to face them.

And then Paul caught up to him with the force of a freight train.

He tackled Larry and as they both hit the ground, the gun fell out of Larry's hand. They rolled apart and Paul, lying on his back, slipped his .45 out of its holster, but Larry recovered, ran over, and kicked it out of his hand before he could react. Why he had holstered the gun in the first place or failed to unholster it as he got closer to Larry was the question Paul was now asking himself as he fought for his life. Words Evelyn had hurled at him more than once came rushing back to him: '*Paul, you're a lawyer, not a killer!*' And she was right.

Paul got to his feet and the two men circled each other briefly before Larry charged Paul. Paul pivoted to one side and caught Larry with an elbow to the base of his neck and he fell to the ground, groggy and listless.

Evelyn and Jean rushed over to where the two men were fighting and circled behind Larry, who, still groggy, struggled to his knees facing the condo. Paul renewed the contest, advancing toward Larry while the women cautiously approached him from behind, waiting for a chance to pounce. Larry, however, managed to get to his feet before anyone got close enough to restrain him. While he stood on wobbly legs, still trying to shake off the effects of the blow to the back of his neck, his pursuers had lost their advantage. They all stopped as though they'd reached the edge of a cliff.

Larry was raising his .45 unsteadily from his side.

By chance, he had fallen on the gun moments earlier when the blow from Paul's elbow forced him to the ground and, in the commotion, no one had noticed. Now Larry, barely ten feet away, took two staggering steps in Paul's direction while holding the .45 in one hand and pressing the palm of his hand against his forehead with the other as he strained mightily to bring Paul into focus.

Panicked and unsure what she could do, Evelyn's eyes darted wildly in every direction. Then they came to rest on something at her feet.

It was Paul's .45.

Silently, she stooped and scooped the gun up.

His back facing the street, Larry stumbled, almost losing his balance. Then, he stopped, and tried to steady himself. Abruptly, he took his hand away from his forehead and grasped the base of the .45 beneath his other hand. He raised his arms, leveling the gun at Paul's chest. His arms were steady. No one spoke. Paul's eyes widened but then a feeling of calm washed over him. He stared at Larry's .45 and breathed deeply. Larry loomed in front of him and blocked his view of Evelyn. His lips pulled back in a sneer.

She had never held a gun, much less fired one. She had heard that some handguns were equipped with something called a "safety," but she had no idea what it looked like, where to find it, or how to use it, assuming this gun had one. If it did, she prayed it was off. She pointed the .45 at Larry's back and put her finger on the trigger.

But a shot rang out before she could fire the gun.

"Oh, no! she screamed. *'I waited too long.'* She closed her eyes, which were flooded with tears, and dropped to her knees on the grass. Blocking out thoughts of what Larry might do next, she let the .45 fall to the ground.

Also teary-eyed, Jean helped her to her feet and gently hugged her. "It's all over," she whispered reassuringly.

Before she could react, Paul hurried up to her. Sensing his presence, through her tears, she opened her eyes, wide with shock, for the first time since she'd heard the shot that she thought had killed him. Jean stepped aside and Evelyn flew into his arms. "Hey, I'm still here," he said, brushing away her tears. Overcome with emotion, she said nothing, just held him tightly, small sobs escaping her as her body shook.

Moments later Rico limped up to join them. Jean, now crying tears of joy, ran up to embrace him. He accepted her embrace, holding her in the safe circle of his arms, and she dried her tears on his shoulder.

"Thanks – again," Paul said to Rico. "For the umpteenth time. I don't know what else to say."

The scuffle between him and Larry had bought Rico enough time to get close enough to take the shot that killed Larry. It had been a tough one. Evelyn and Jean had been standing behind Larry, shoulder to shoulder with only inches between them. In order to hit Larry, Rico's bullet had to travel between the narrow space separating the two women. Once it cleared that space, it had entered the back of Larry's head and exited through his eye.

"You don't hafta say anything," Rico said to Paul. "Maybe she coulda pulled the trigger, but better me than her."

"You mean?" Evelyn stammered, fresh tears streaming down her cheeks.

"Yes," Jean said, stepping out of Rico's embrace as if on cue.

Evelyn spontaneously hugged him then, catching him by surprise, before stepping back, a little self-consciously. Then she immediately hugged Jean once more. Jean winked at Rico, who said nothing. But he winked back.

He was curious about something. He hobbled over to where Paul's .45 lay and picked it up. "Interesting," he said out loud.

The safety was on.

He handed the gun to Paul who had walked over to join him. "Like I said, better me than her." He gave a little nod.

Rico couldn't bear to have Paul believe he was indebted to Rico. Several months earlier Paul had wounded a man who was trying to kill him. The man had stumbled out of Paul's apartment still very much alive. Outside he had encountered Rico, who shot him dead. Although Paul later learned the truth, Rico, not wanting Paul to feel he owed Rico anything, had let Paul believe that Paul had fired the fatal shot. Now, he wanted Paul to believe that if he had not intervened and shot Larry, Evelyn could have done so without any help from him.

Paul checked the safety.

It was off.

When Gus left the house the first time, his wife had had a premonition that something terrible would happen to him, and she'd paced the floor until he returned unharmed. She hadn't felt physically tired, but the weight of her worry had been oppressive, and she'd felt emotionally drained. So relieved had she been upon his safe return, that despite not feeling sleepy, her eyelids had grown heavy, like leaden weights, and she'd fallen fast asleep on the sofa with her head on Gus's shoulder.

Surprisingly, she hadn't had a second premonition when she awakened around midnight to find Gus gone with no explanation. Indeed, she'd been remarkably free of worry. The first premonition had been so strong that she'd been unable to muster the emotional energy necessary to sustain a second one. As more and more time passed, however, she'd begun to fret. Gus didn't like it when he was out, and she called his cell for anything other than an emergency of some sort. Since she didn't even have a premonition any longer, of course, there was no emergency.

Finally, at daybreak, she could wait no longer. She'd called again and again, and again and again the call had gone straight to voice mail until, finally, his mailbox was full. She had not gone to bed all night and she still didn't have a premonition. She just thought Gus had been delayed for some reason, which wasn't unusual. When she could think of nothing else to do, she went to the front window and stood there peering out at the cold, gray dawn. She would still be standing there on aching legs when the police arrived some two hours later to ask her to come with them to identify Gus's body.

Carrying her cell phone, Sadie had already called 911 by the time she descended the stairs in a mad rush to get to Cleveland. From her vantage point, the driver of the car had been hidden by the roof of his car, just as Gus had suspected. But despite having seen him for only a second or two, ironically, she'd recognized Larry as an infrequent customer at her drug store. She gave that information to the two policemen who interviewed her at the hospital as she sat on a sofa in the patient lounge, quietly sobbing. Bright and early the next day they started asking quietly around the neighborhood and soon found out who Larry was. The next morning Sadie identified his photo at the hospital, where she'd spent the night. Gus would have been most surprised.

The two officers were still there when a doctor entered the room wearing familiar green scrubs and confirmed that Sadie was the woman who had been waiting for news about Cleveland. She told him that she was the one he was looking for, then sprang to her feet and hurried to him, stopping only about a foot away. Her heart sank, though, when she saw his somber expression.

But he was somber by nature. "He's a very lucky man," the doctor said in serious tones. "He'll need lots of time to recuperate, but he's going to pull through. I suspect that something in the trash bags absorbed some of the force of the bullets."

Sadie swooned and the doctor caught her. "Here, here," he said. "Are you all right?"

"Yes, I'm fine," Sadie said, recovering. "I'm so relieved. Can I see him?"

"A little later."

Distracted, Sadie said, "I'll have to call the funeral home."

"I guess you didn't have very much faith in us," the doctor said, smiling.

"No, not for Cleveland. For his brother. His funeral was supposed to be today. Just think. We almost had to bury him, too." Tears sprang afresh to her red eyes.

"Well, you won't have to worry about that for a long time, I hope. Incidentally, he was conscious for a moment before we took him to surgery, and he asked me to tell you something. He said to tell you not to worry and that he "got out." I hope that means something to you."

"It does. A lot."

Chapter Twenty-Five

For once, Rico stuck around and waited for the police. Despite his long life of crime, he had never even been arrested. In part that was because he never left any clues – or witnesses if it came to that. It was also due in part to the fact that, apart from the time he was ambushed by Larry's buddies outside the supermarket, he'd always been long gone by the time the police arrived. Certainly, as he'd told Lieutenant Cannon, they knew all too well who he was. But neither they nor the State's Attorney could ever pin anything on him.

A neighbor had dialed 911 shortly after Rico's car slammed into the one carrying Gus, Larry, and the other two goons. The police didn't arrive, though, until about five minutes after Rico killed Larry. That gave the survivors time to decide what they would say.

This was tricky for Paul. As an attorney, he was an officer of the court, and as such, he couldn't lie to or mislead the police, nor counsel anyone else to do so. Technically, he was not the attorney for Rico, Jean, or Evelyn. They had not retained him, there was no attorney client privilege between him and them, and he couldn't counsel them as their attorney. He could, however, give them general advice, which he did.

He told them to listen carefully to each question asked, to make sure they understood it before they answered, not to guess at answers, and to only respond to the question asked as succinctly as possible. He also told them that they need not volunteer any information that wasn't responsive to a specific question. Finally, he told them that as an officer of the court, he intended to tell the truth and recommended that they do so as well, within the guidelines he had given them.

This was essentially what Paul counseled clients and witnesses all the time, except that he didn't *recommend* that his clients tell the truth. He *instructed* them to do so, even if it hurt. Bad things can happen during cross-examination but getting caught in a lie is not one of them if you always tell the truth.

What made Paul's advice tricky was that, unlike in his law practice, here he was a participant in the events. In his law practice a client or a witness would be free to testify that X had taken place even if there was evidence that in fact Y had taken place, and, *because he did not witness what happened*, as an attorney, Paul could choose to believe that X had taken place if X was what favored his client. Conversely, *if Paul were himself a witness*, he could not argue as a lawyer that X had taken place when he himself saw Y take place, even if his client testified that X had taken place. For that reason, with rare exceptions, a lawyer cannot represent a client in a matter where the lawyer may be called as a witness. He needed to be very careful.

After Paul paused to let his explanation sink in, Rico said, "So you told us how to answer questions, and you recommended that we tell the truth. You wanna break that down a little more?"

"Yes, I should have," Paul said. "I think we should tell them that we were having dinner after we read about Mr. Koblentz's death in the paper. I'm sure they'll ask for statements, and we should start there. Afterwards, we realized that Jean might also be in danger, so Evelyn asked her to spend the night at our condo. Meanwhile, I took you to pick up your car where Jean had left it when the three of us picked her up to drive to the restaurant together. On the way we realized that Jean might be in just as much danger at my condo if someone figured she might go there instead of to her apartment. We raced back there and any of us can describe exactly what happened. Of course, it's self-evident that we acted in self-defense."

"That leaves a lot out," Jean said.

"I know," Paul said. "But since Jean's kidnapping and Rico subsequent rescue of her and everything leading up to that part of the story are incidental to what just happened here, I'm hoping there won't be a reason to bring it up. We need to leave Buster out of things, too, if we can."

"It's messy, I know," Evelyn said. "But no one here did anything wrong or anything to be ashamed of." She had pulled herself together once it was clear that Paul was unharmed and was now calm and resolute. Evelyn glanced at Rico and added, "I don't know what happened in that café, but I'm sure whatever happened was necessary to save Jean."

"You don't wanna know either," Rico said. "But you're right."

"Everybody's right," Paul said. "Remember, we're not trying to hide anything. We're just trying to keep this as simple as possible. All that's really important is that four men tried to kidnap or kill us and that we defended ourselves and killed them instead. These men had been holding a grudge and seeking revenge ever since that incident outside the supermarket. We're just lucky they didn't succeed and that we came out on top."

"Hear, hear," Rico said.

"And if they want to know any details about what happened before dinner, I'll have to answer truthfully and again, I recommend that everyone else do the same. As you said, Evelyn and I don't know what happened inside the café, so we can't support or contradict anything you say. Maybe it won't come up. Is that okay with everyone?"

Evelyn and Jean nodded their approval. Rico understood Paul's predicament and reacted with characteristic aplomb. "You do what you gotta do, counselor, and I'll do what I gotta do."

It was a risky strategy because there was a good chance that their statements, if examined closely, would be viewed as rehearsed and, therefore, potentially untruthful. Paul hoped that because the four of them were so clearly the innocent victims of known criminals, the police would view their statements as merely pro forma and wouldn't see the need to examine them in any great detail.

When police arrived, they found Paul, Rico, Evelyn, and Jean sitting on the curb in front of the condo. The police loaded each of them into separate squad cars and obtained preliminary accounts of what took place. Then they drove everyone to the police station and each of them gave a formal written statement to a different detective. As they'd discussed, everyone started their statement with the dinner.

Shortly after they gave their statements, everyone was released without further questioning, but all was not well. While the police hadn't asked about anything that happened before the dinner, the lead detective, Sergeant Muller, a lean, wiry man in his late thirties with a blond crewcut, pulled Paul aside and made it clear to him that they were just getting started with their investigation. He added that despite the fact that the victims were known felons who didn't evoke much sympathy, at this early stage of the investigation, the police didn't view what happened as an open and shut case of self-defense. Ominously, he also said that while no one was being charged that night, it wasn't a certainty that no one would be charged in the future. Finally, Muller told Paul that he might want to consider discussing with the others whether they should consult a criminal lawyer. Paul scoffed at that notion, but he was not pleased.

The only thing Paul shared with the others was that the police would have to do some further investigation, which he described as "routine". It had been a long night. He suggested that they all go home and get a good night's sleep and reconvene at his office the next day. No one objected.

Paul arrived at his office early and started thinking about criminal lawyers he could consult with. He didn't think that ultimately anyone would be charged, but things could get messy. On reflection, it was clear to him that a good criminal lawyer could help to limit the fallout. He had someone in mind but before reaching out to him, he called Sgt. Muller for an update. He was pleasantly surprised.

He waited until everyone arrived to share the news with them. Evelyn got there first and pulled up a chair alongside Paul, who sat behind his desk. Rico and Jean arrived together about five minutes after Evelyn and sat on the leather sofa in front of Paul's desk. After greeting everyone, he glanced at Rico. "I didn't know you had any connections in the police department," he quipped. "How long did you plan on keeping that a secret?"

"Trust me, counselor, I have about as much pull down there as Al Capone had."

"I didn't want anybody to lose any sleep last night, so I didn't tell you that Sgt. Muller told me that this investigation was just getting started and that I might want to discuss with the three of you whether we should retain criminal counsel. Well, thanks to Mr. Sanders here, we no longer have to worry about that."

Evelyn and Jean both turned to Rico, anticipating an explanation.

"Don't look at me," Rico said.

"Paul, will you please tell us what happened?" Evelyn said anxiously.

Jean took Rico's hand in hers and squeezed it tightly.

"Muller said a Lieutenant Cannon pulled rank on him and ordered him to shut the investigation down. According to Cannon, the evidence showed that we were good Samaritans who clearly acted in self-defense, and any additional investigation would be a waste of the taxpayers' money. Cannon also asked him to deliver a message to Mr. Sanders. He said to tell you that he hopes your leg is better and that you don't develop a limp."

Everyone glanced at Rico and awaited his response. All he said was, "That makes two of us."

Once everyone got over the shock from Paul's surprise announcement, he gave them one more bit of news. "After he told me they were dropping the investigation, Muller told me something he'd found out before Cannon pulled him off the case. In a way, we did the police a favor. It turns out they were already out looking for the two men inside the car we rammed. Attempted murder of a man named Cleveland Russell. Wasn't Russell the name of one of the men –"

"Yeah, his brother," Rico said.

"Why would they want to kill him?"

"Bad blood. They tried to pin Gabe Koblentz's murder on him."

Paul stood, stepped in front of his desk, and leaned back against it with his hands clasped in front of him. "Anyway, I guess that just about covers everything."

"I've never even been arrested, let alone released on my own recognizance," Rico mused. "How about you, counselor?"

"Afraid not," Paul said. He thought for a moment. "What would you have done if I hadn't still been there when you came back last night? You wouldn't have known how to get to my house, would you?"

"No, but I would have figured it out eventually. Anyway, I was pretty sure you'd still be there."

"But what if I hadn't?" he persisted.

Rico glanced discreetly at Evelyn. "He knew you would," she said. "And so did I."

"Lucky for us you were," Jean said.

"How did they connect me to you?" Paul asked Rico.

"Gus – or somebody workin' with him – must have followed Jean that day when she came here to see you. Right after she came back, Gus asked me - all casual - if you handle divorce cases. That gave him away. It was a dumb thing to say. He thought I knew she'd been here, and I guess he wanted to see if I'd blink."

"He assumed that I was hiding you?"

"Maybe. But he didn't care where I was, as long as he thought he had Larry under control. Then the shit hit the fan – pardon my French – and he found out Larry had screwed him. His sister must have had him in a real hammerlock, 'cause after all that, he decided he wasn't gonna give Larry up after he told me he would. That's when he gambled that we'd come back to your place."

Rico's leg was bothering him a little. He stood, leaned against his cane, and emitted a small sigh of relief. Jean asked him, "If Gus knew I had been here to see Paul, how did you know he wouldn't make the connection to the cabin and come out there?"

"'Cause he meant it when he said he'd worked out a truce, so he didn't have any reason to try to find me or to come lookin' for me if he did."

"But how did you know Larry didn't know about me?" Paul asked Rico.

"Truce or no truce, Gus would never have told him. It would be like dangling a piece of raw meat in front of a jackal and expectin' him to walk away from it."

"But suppose it wasn't Gus, but Larry or someone working with him who followed Jean?" Paul asked.

"Larry didn't have any self-control – or brains," Rico said. "Him or anybody he sent woulda done somethin' stupid, like tryin' to grab you, counselor, or maybe Jean, which, if you remember, is what he finally did try."

"And I suppose you didn't change your mind about going to the cabin at the last minute because you really wanted to spend some time in the country," Jean said reproachfully.

Rico eased back into his seat on the sofa. "I did wanna spend some time out there," he said. "But I also didn't want to be recoverin' at my place and you gettin' caught in the middle. I was pretty sure he wouldn't find out about the cabin, but I knew he could find out when I was gettin' out of the hospital."

There was a knock at the door. Paul went and opened it. It was Bryson Barnes. "I'm sorry to interrupt," he said coldly. "But can I see you for a moment?"

Paul excused himself and stepped into the hall outside his office. Although he closed the door behind him, it remained slightly ajar. He and Barnes stood toe to toe facing each other with only a few feet separating them.

"I don't know quite how to put this," Barnes said. His voice had a distinct edge to it. "You've seen the morning paper?"

"I have."

"We just talked about this and you told me not to worry. Well, I'm worried now. I don't have to tell you that this law firm doesn't need this kind of publicity – especially after the negative press you've generated over the past few years."

"Well, you keep calling it negative, but you know that, in fact, most of it has been positive. Each time there was press, I was trying to save my life or somebody else's. But what's done is done," Paul said, a little defensively. "I'm sorry about the part that has been negative, and I'm sorry I couldn't keep a lid on this like I told you I would, but things just spun out of control."

Paul thought that his apology for something that wasn't actually his fault would be acknowledged, at least in passing, but Barnes plowed ahead, undeterred. "I seem to recall things spinning out of control twice before over the last couple of years."

Paul's jaw tightened and he narrowed his eyes. Trying to hold it together, he took a step back and folded his arms across his chest. "You have an excellent memory."

Barnes's eyes widened then flickered. Taken aback, he was both surprised and upset at what he viewed as a challenge to his authority. "Look here," he said, his voice rising an octave. "I'm trying to be diplomatic about this."

Paul refused to back down. "Fine," he said. "You've made your point. Now, is there anything else?"

"Yes, as a matter of fact. I think it's unseemly for that man and his girlfriend to be lounging around our offices."

Paul, who was standing with his back to his office turned and glanced behind him. "They're hardly lounging around."

"In any event, I think it would be wise if they left – and didn't come back."

His frustration mounting, Paul said, "Bryson, I've tried to keep in mind that you're the managing partner of this office, and that you're acting in what you think is the best interest of the firm. But I think you're out of line."

"Oh, you do, do you?

"Yes, I do. *'That man'* as you call him, saved my life – three times now."

Barnes didn't have a comeback, except to end the conversation. "Do you intend to ask him to leave or not?"

"Rico stays."

"What?" Barnes said, not understanding, his eyes glaring at Paul's defiance.

"His name is Rico and he stays."

"We'll see about that."

Barnes turned to walk away. As he did, Paul said, "You can see all you want, but you don't have the votes."

Paul had not wanted a showdown but now that it had happened, he was glad to be done with it. While his activities had indeed generated some negative publicity, as he'd said, most of it had been either neutral or favorable. And as for Rico, he had never been arrested or charged with any crime associated with his encounters with Paul. In fact, although there had been rumors and innuendos, the one incident that the police and the newspapers were aware of that involved Rico was the shootout outside Paul and Evelyn's condo the night before.

From the moment Paul's name started to appear in the newspapers, he had kept a number of his partners in the loop and explained, to the extent he felt necessary, the unusual circumstances under which incidents of violence had suddenly become a part of his life. He had omitted some crucial details, principally those involving his and Evelyn's first encounter with Rico in Honolulu. That would have been harder to explain but since almost no one knew about it except him and Evelyn, there was no reason for anyone else to know.

It was true that he had now killed two men outright and, with Rico's participation, probably a third. And it was true that it was more than a little unusual for a buttoned-down lawyer at a large, respected law firm to have that kind of history. But it was also true that each of the men in question had been a murderer who had been trying to kill him, Rico, or an innocent teenage girl. Under those circumstances, to many of his law partners, Paul was a kind of reluctant hero through whose exploits, subconsciously at least, some of them lived vicariously, not unlike the way Paul subconsciously lived through Rico's exploits. In a dispute with Barnes, these partners would certainly side with Paul.

He watched Barnes until he reached the end of the hall before he opened the door to his office. Seeing everyone standing and facing the door, he hesitated a moment before closing it, and then sheepishly straightened his tie. "Well, where were we?" he asked.

"Paul, the door wasn't quite closed," Evelyn said. "We heard everything."

"You didn't have to do that for me, counselor," Rico said.

"I didn't do it for you," Paul said, slightly embarrassed. I did it for Jean – and for me."

"Thanks, Paul," Jean said, her cheeks pink.

Evelyn came over and gave him a hug. "I don't always agree with you…"

"You're allowed," Paul said.

"But I'm proud of you, Paul," Evelyn finished.

Paul exited Evelyn's embrace, took a step backward, and gazed at her admiringly. Taking her by the hand, he said to the others, "Excuse us for a minute." He led her into the hall and closed his office door, this time making sure it was closed all the way. "I have a surprise for you when we get home," he confided. "It rhymes with "sing" and starts with the letter "r."

Evelyn's eyes brightened. "Oh, Paul!"

She gave him a passionate kiss and, both of them beaming, they returned to his office. When they entered, not waiting for a question, Paul said, "Our secret."

"Far be it from us to say anything," Rico said, raising his hands.

Jean guessed and her face lit up with delight. She hurried over to Evelyn and whispered in her ear, "Congratulations!"

Rico looked on silently, stoically, his arms folded across his chest. Jean returned to his side, took his hand in hers, and gazed up at him expectantly. He bent down and kissed her lightly on the lips, and gently stroked the side of her face. She smiled and ducked under his arm, tucking herself in against his side, which was enough for her.

Paul looked around, his gaze taking everyone in but resting finally on Rico. "All good?"

"All good, counselor," Rico said.

"Somehow I don't think we'll ever be drinking buddies," Paul said.

"You're right," Rico said, deadpan. "I pick my drinking buddies better than that."

"But if I call you 'Rico,' do you think you could drop the 'counselor' and call me 'Paul?'"

"I think that might be arranged."

THE END

Dear reader,

We hope you enjoyed reading *Rico Stays*. Please take a moment to leave a review, even if it's a short one. Your opinion is important to us.

Discover more books by Ed Duncan at
https://www.nextchapter.pub/authors/author-ed-duncan

Want to know when one of our books is free or discounted? Join the newsletter at http://eepurl.com/bqqB3H

Best regards,

Ed Duncan and the Next Chapter Team

You could also like:
Sealing Fate by David P. Warren

To read the first chapter for free, please head to:
https://www.nextchapter.pub/books/sealing-fate

About the Author

Ed is a graduate of Oberlin College and Northwestern University Law School. He was a partner at a national law firm in Cleveland, Ohio for many years. He is the original author of a highly regarded legal treatise entitled *Ohio Insurance Coverage*, for which he provided annual editions from 2008 through 2012. *Rico Stays* is the third novel in the *Pigeon-Blood Red Trilogy* which began with *Pigeon-Blood Red* and was followed by *The Last Straw*. Ed, originally from Gary, Indiana, lives outside Cleveland.

Rico Stays
ISBN: 978-4-86750-227-3

Published by
Next Chapter
1-60-20 Minami-Otsuka
170-0005 Toshima-Ku, Tokyo
+818035793528
7th June 2021

CPSIA information can be obtained
at www.ICGtesting.com
Printed in the USA
BVHW031702280621
610633BV00004B/867